N

# N

## Phase 03 of The Renpet Phenomenon

## DjaDja N-Medjay



Contact the author at: th3rp1@gmail.com

and therenpetphenom.com

Printed in the United States of America.

ISBN

N

*Other titles by DjaDja Medjay*
***Renpet***
***Rising Depth***

## *Chapter Wa*
## *Powder*

I kept staring at the their unconscious bodies, piled over each other in the thick patch of small plants. The makeshift club—that the more aggressive of the two swung at us—now sat idly next to their musky bodies.

An urge to pick it up and bash them with it, ran through my arms, causing my hands to twitch.

"Leave that—and them—alone." Mother's sharp tone snapped me out of my trance, just as I reached down to pick-up the club. "Let's go…*now,*" she commanded.

I reluctantly turned away from them and followed her lead, eventually catching up to walk by her side. Gradually, the rage that I'd carried with me since I was a child, mellowed out with the rhythmic sound of the rain's heavy drops against the canopy of soft leaves above us.

"We make choices, Jnf," She paused, pulled her swollen

hand away from the cart and rubbed it along her thigh. "Choices do not make us," she finished and placed her hand back on the cart handle.

Mother didn't speak after that, but she kept her conversation going with the heaviness her steps made on the ground. She usually never made a sound when walking through the woods. But today, I heard every leaf she made contact with.

* * *

The moment Mother and I stepped from out of the woods into the clearing that lead into the city, the heavy rainfall that had fiercely battered leaves and branches struck us head-on. Instead of being caught by the tops of trees, its huge drops pummeled the paved black granite streets of Nkh Nwt.

I sensed Mother's small mental impulse to the portion of our Hn symbiote Mu; which lived in the bone marrow of our arms.

Mu projected a covering large enough to shield our lop-sided cart, that contained fresh meat from our recent catch. Our monthly meat delivery to the famous deli, *The Taste,* wouldn't get its full tkkn worth if tampered with.

Of course, she didn't seem to care to have that same

projection expand over *us*, to keep us dry too. And I wasn't permitted to do so either.

"Time and time again I've instructed you to manage your skhm, and keep calm when approached with aggression." She broke the silence between us, but still didn't make eye contact with me.

"Yes, Mother." I hung my head low.

"Yes, Mother *what?* You apologize for provoking those lazy thieves in the woods? Or do you apologize for that fact that I had to handle them, since I forbade you to fight." She looked at me with annoyance. I kept my mouth shut. There was nothing I could say in my defense.

"In any case, that little situation cost us time. I wanted to be in and out of the city before it started to rain heavy." She relaxed the tension in her face. "Oh well, it cannot be helped."

Before I allowed Mother's words to further take hold of my mood, I turned my attention to the streets that rippled out in a beautiful gleam wherever the raindrops fell. No matter how much the sky filled with gray clouds, there was no way it could dampen my love of the city.

As we walked pass the corner of Nb Avenue and Snb Street, workers from various guilds— mostly the Htp Guild— dashed under whatever awning they could to stay dry. And as usual, rank determined who would remain under the awning and who would stand out in the rain waiting to attend to them.

A Master Guildsman strolled by, and directed his Hn to shake out the water from his umbrella and close back into The Fold, before he anxiously slid into the huddle of people. Workers who were a part of his guild, stumbled over each other to offer him their spot, before they meekly stood out in the rain.

Mother openly sucked her teeth, and glared at him with scorn. She thought it was a waste of energy to harness the relationship between Hn and their hosts for trivial things like that. *We* were getting soaked.

Yet, I didn't mind so much. While we walked through the empty wet streets, I felt like we were on display for all the people crowded in front of stores and station stops.

She tried to pull me along by my arm while pushing the cart at the same time. But I didn't budge. My arm slipped out her grasp, while she tried to manage the cart. It was just about impossible to get me to move *and* push the cart efficiently—especially with one of the hover beams practically busted.

"I am not going to ruin my favorite dress because of your girlish whims," she said irritatingly. "Neither I am in the mood to set you straight. Get drenched, if that is your wish!" She raced across the street to shelter with the cart.

# N

The heavy sigh that flew out my mouth, would have blown into her face if she hadn't darted off so quick—which was fortunate for me. My body still ached in places from the last time she *set me straight.*

While I leaned up against the nearby lamppost on the corner and looked up into the sky, the coldness of its stone surface sent shivers into my spine. For a brief moment, sunlight poured down on my face, but it wasn't too long before the clouds covered it again.

Despite the rain, wonderful smells swirled about me...the musk of people, the scents of sulfur from the sparks of Tkkn, and the freshly treated woody fragrances of the buildings; most of them anyway.

A few people who ran past, glanced at me as if I were crazy or something. "Mind your own damn business!" I yelled at them, frustrated that they were interrupting my peace.

"Still enjoying yourself?" Mother called out from across the street.

No, I wasn't. *Seems like the downpours are the same no matter where you are. Damn!*

At this point, nothing was enjoyable about being soaked from head to toe. The intricate parts in my braids, that mother had painstakingly created, were now frizzy and frayed.

My clothes clung to my breasts and hips: showing off just how much I was coming off age. And as if that wasn't enough, some boy kept inching up closer and closer to me.

He was big, but didn't have a threatening look about him. Yet I could tell he was up to something, by the way he kept fidgeting every time I looked in his direction.

*Doesn't matter.*

I turned my attention to how the rain had let up some while the scents around me became stronger— more recognizable. I loved the city; it was the exact change of pace needed from forest life.

While I was daydreaming, that boy was able to get within a few feet of me. *Finally, a chance to let off some steam!*

Almost immediately out the corner of my eye, I caught mother stomping her foot in irritation, and then swiftly making her way over to me. Just as she moved in between us, the boy pulled out a long knife.

All I saw was the bright orange flash of mother's house-dress, when the attacker lunged at her with his blade—I think he wanted me instead. The knife missed mother's chest but continued for my throat. My heart raced when the tip lightly grazed my skin, just before I leapt back.

It didn't seem to register with him, how easily Mother

dodged the blade by stepping to his left side. Maybe he thought he'd already stabbed her, because he had a look of surprise when he saw my face instead of hers.

More than likely he depended on his size to strike fear in his victims, and carried the knife more for show than cutting. I guess he didn't count on using it when he underestimated mother's size.

I'm sure that the crowd that gathered around us thought the same way. Her small frame and elegant movement, didn't give much of an impression of a fighter.

*She has to finish this quick though—it's not good to fight in a closed space like this.*

Anyway, leaving our cart unattended might invite thieves, who'd take our prize catch of meat before we could make it to the butcher.

*Nnnngh! I am sooo tempted to reach out and choke this fool into oblivion just to get this over with! But I don't know how many of his friends may be around waiting for an opportunity to jump in.*

So many people in the crowd made it difficult to discern sudden, aggressive movement and their individual scents seem to blend into one another even in the light rain.

*Weaklings. All they want is to be able to experience something they know they can't do themselves.*

He was so slow in processing a combat situation, that I was able to ramble on in my thoughts *and* assess our surroundings well before he finally caught on.

Anyhow, mother just took advantage of his lack of balance, by stepping in from his side onto his knee. She brought her full body weight down on it. He toppled over sideways towards the street's cobblestone ground—the cracking sound of his knee being displaced, rang out loudly.

He tried to break his fall but ended up stabbing himself in the leg instead—completely forgetting what was still clutched in his hand, he hysterically yelled out in pain and distress.

Mother, who followed the motion of his falling, yanked out the knife stuck in his leg and scampered up his body just as he hit the ground.

She brought the blade to his neck and sighed. "It's evident that my actions will eventually lead to your need for vengeance and I really don't wish to release your spirit."

"What I am to do?" Mother spoke even-toned and as curt as possible.

*I already know where this is going, better get the* poison powder *ready for her.* The fearsome look painted across this fool's face earlier, had completely washed away.

"Jnf stop daydreaming and check on the cart." Mother

scolded me, while keeping the boy still.

I looked up and down the street and saw that Kvn had pushed our cart into an alley, and was standing next to it. He'd made sure the cart was secure while we were in the skirmish. I didn't sense that he was in the area earlier. He shielded himself on purpose just to irritate me. Kvn re-stabilized the hover streams on it, then walked over to me.

*I know what's on his mind... its all in his scent.*

He reached out and grabbed me, pulling me into the alley where the cart was. Of course I could have gotten free at any time—I wanted to see where this would lead to *this* time.

He pushed me against the wall to make his usual advances; although he could have picked a better place to grope on me. Did he think that amongst the stacks of recycling paper and smells from the restaurant vents, I would give into him freely…?

*Right.* At least he was considerate enough to keep me within sight and earshot of mother.

He sniffed along my neck, brushing the tip of his nose against my skin and breathing lightly. My heart wanted to leap out from my chest, yet I had to control its rhythm.

I needed him inside me but he was still too young in mind and spirit, and the same could be said for me.

Kvn pulled me close to him and embraced me. When the

pressure of his hug became more than a friendly squeeze, I felt my hair stand on end and looked up into the sky. I gasped as I dropped my neck back and pointed my chin upwards.

Arching forward this way, intensified the feeling in my chest as my breasts pushed into his chest. Scattered rain drops hit my cheeks—the moisture matching the one building in between my legs.

He pressed his palms into my back, stroking them down the outside of my spine, following the curve of my body.

*Mmmmmm. Maybe if I let him….no, too soon.*

"Get off me!" I said as sternly as I could, without bruising his ego. When I pushed him back, he extended his neck close enough to be able to lick my collar-bone ever so gently. I punched him in the right side of his rib cage just below his lungs.

When reached for his chest and opened his mouth to take a deep breath, I thrust my tongue into his mouth and licked his tongue. Through this brief connection of fluids, I told him my feelings, as did he.

Then I slapped him on top of his head. Our saliva had grown more and more electrically stimulated, each time we kissed during these encounters. He fell to the ground on his backside looking up at me smiling ear to ear.

Kvn was by far no slouch with his hands—his slim but muscular frame always fooled lames who tested his ability. Too many times, he left these types of idiots laid out the ground: holding a swollen head and cupping their bloody nose.

Yet, Kvn never looked for trouble. *I guess that's one reason I always mess with him...to see how good he really is.*

"Jnf, the blade," mother called out to me

That's my cue.

"See you tomorrow Jnfr?" Kvn called out to me as I left him on sitting on the ground.

"Don't go nowhere. Watch that cart and maybe I'll see," I replied in my most enticing voice, seeing that it gave him some hope.

When I got over to mother she gave me a look of disgust that slowly changed to a look of understanding.

"Are you done getting felt up? Idiot. Get to work." She said in a confusing voice.

*I'm lucky that she's preoccupied.* I returned a look of humility, and sprinkled just enough powder on the surface of the blade.

*We've had so many threats and extortion attempts, we only have a little left. As the wet season approaches, it will be more difficult to find the necessary herbs for the mixture.*

"No, no please let me go! I don't want to die *Please...!*" the big thug pleaded for his life, while passing gas from fear.

"Shh, shh...Be quiet. Don't move" mother commanded, fully playing off his anxiety.

She stroked his low crop of tight curls, to his nape; then suddenly grabbed him by the back of his neck, digging into his flesh with her fingernails.

"This is going to sting…just a bit."

His body tensed up in anticipation of what she was going to do. He couldn't keep still and began kicking his feet— his heels scuffing across the wet ground. Even worst for him, her hands were getting wet from the rain. So she had to constantly re-adjust her grip, making more fresh cuts around his neck.

"Don't move...I am quick enough to grant you release in a fraction of a second." She yanked his head back and looked coldly into his eyes.

He began to calm down and submit to her. As soon as I rolled up the sleeve of his shirt, mother ran the blade across his arm: opening up his flesh just enough so that the powder would enter his bloodstream.

"Forgive me for being impolite and not asking your name. What do they call you?"

"R-r-r-km", he muttered softly, trying to hold in his panic.

"Rkm, before I let you go let me explain to you what has

happened and what *will* happen..." Mother went on to tell him that his life now belonged to her... that he was poisoned with a near incurable concoction.

And only she possessed the antidote. She said that if he valued his life that he would not make any more threats on our lives or others. In exchange, she would gradually administer the cure whenever she visited the city.

*In truth, there's no poison in that mixture. In fact it detoxifies the anger of impure emotions. I must admit this whole scheme that mother cooked up comes in handy.*

We'd come across many idiots like this one, who wanted to extort us for the Tkkn we are paid for selling freshly hunted animal meat, to the leading butcher shops in the city.

Our catch always got good payment, because of the way we cleansed the meat of spirits that might resent being released from their bodies. Our natural way of hunting preserved the vitality and taste of our catch.

*Predators think that since we live in the woods, we're easy prey under the dim-lit streets on the path out of the city. But what made this fool think he would have more success in the late afternoon—when there is still light in the sky?*

Ironically, all the thugs that attacked us, later thanked us for curing them of their inflictions, and setting them on the right path.

This one that mother left sitting on the curb, was already showing a look of remorse on his face. *He will be no different from the others.*

The crowd slowly broke up their gathering—some walking away displeased that there wasn't more bloodshed.

*Fools. They forget how the All Nature rewards those who shed too much unwarranted blood.*

For that reason, the residents living the street life seemed to have the worst memory of this known law. Most of them met their end, as soon as they fell out of balance.

"Jnfr stop your daydreaming. Let's finish up here so we can get home in good time." Mother demanded. "Set his knee." She motioned to his leg that lay limp on the street.

Suddenly the rain became heavy and battered his face, washing tears away.

"Hold still Rkm." I managed to speak gently to him although, everything inside of me wanted to do otherwise.

'O-o-oKay..." he said sheepishly.

"On three," I whispered. "Three." I called nonchalantly, and snapped his bone back into place.

He looked at me like I'd betrayed his trust, yet somehow held back his anguish.

"You'll be alright! Now get out of here!" Before I finished my sentence, he was already on his feet hobbling off.

"What's happening in the sky?" someone yelled, pointing over their head.

"It's opening *up!"* another screamed.

The sky turned an indigo-red and the lining on the clouds became menacingly dark. I have never seen anything like it nor *felt* anything like it before.

I felt pressure from the sky—like something was invading my body.

Something foreign.

People in the street screamed in panic, and a sea of their outstretched arms pointed to the sky. An object shot out across of the clouds toward the woods, close to the direction of our home. When it hit, everyone was laid to the ground from the tremors.

The rush of uneasy energy from all the creatures of the woods swept through the streets, bombarding everyone's senses.

Mother and I stood steadfast amongst the people around us, staggering in anguish...

# N

## *Chapter Senu*
## *Rebirth*

I'd been transported to another reality. Again. The impact of hitting its surface was the same as hitting the ones before. Painful.

*It seems that the Khemenu Nebu have yet to release me from what they think is my repentance. I wonder, at times, how many of these trials are guided by their personal doing or by cosmic law?*

*I see no difference.*

The MerKaba that dragged me to this place, melted back into my suit as soon as I entered the atmosphere. Dropped several miles out the sky, had literally smashed my body against this world.

My flesh stung all over. Wherever I turned I was greeted by pain. As I struggled to gather my wits, the world around me continued in a whirlwind blur to my vision; while my brain jostled back and forth in my skull.

I was thankful for the moist ground that absorbed my fall, and allowed me to be driven deep into it. Usually my body went naturally limp to avoid adding tension to my joints. Yet this time, as soon as I hit, my muscles self-consciously clutched at the earth—aggressively as if it were an enemy.

The coolness of the soil relaxed my grip. Clumps of earth clung to my palms looking for release. I looked up at my surroundings...There was plush green vegetation that soothed the rush of sekhem that poured into my eyes.

*Whatever is posing a threat is definitely not in the soil… Not physically anyway.* I gave it back to the soil, but not before I rubbed it in between my fingers.

*Time to secure a place to rest and assess my situation, rather than sitting out here in the open.*

I strained every muscle to the bone just to stand and even more to walk. Weakened, my body stumbled into what seemed to be a tree.

As I uncoiled myself from the huge leaves, I saw that it was actually an enormous plant. As I shuffled through the wooded area, the moist cool atmosphere of the shadow hours embraced my body... My senses were now at ease.

# N

*The air here is heavy and seems to almost move away from me as I stride through it. Yet its content doesn't seem to be too difficult to manage, the way it fills and leaves my lungs is invigorating.*

An uneasy tension ran through my legs—something beyond my injuries. Still the modest one-piece battle suit provided by the Khemenu Nebu, seemed to support my body's functions enough to help counteract whatever effect the planet was having on me.

*They must be getting soft in their current cycle of life... This suit shows off my figure as well. I'm getting a little thick in the rear.*

In the past, coming into a new world unclothed, had more than fortified my self-confidence, regardless of my stature as a divine being.

*Rising in nature, eon after eon, leaves no room for stagnant thought patterns (like some people, I've known in the past that struggled with them).*

Yet, there have been lands where the beings— rivaled if not surpassed— my own cosmic awareness. And it was quite humbling, to say the least.

The towering trees stretched towards the early night sky, forever. Their presence blended perfectly with the darkness.

Calmness and drawing in of energies harmonized with the rhythmic, chirping sound of insects in the distance. While the cool air settled into my skin and soothed the spreading fire within, a draw from the soft earth tingled into the soles of my feet.

As my toes pushed into the ground, a voice called out to me. One tree in particular: an elder. Once I found the one that called for me, I stood quietly in front of its immense body and allowed it to *know* me. My left foot found its place in front of my body almost without my thoughts.

I allowed my left arm to follow as the eye of Heru, that rests in my brain, vibrated rapidly...then released its dew into my throat. I swished it around with my saliva. Without words, I breathed out a silent request to sit by its trunk.

A resounding *Yesss* came through the earth into my feet. I held my hand in front of my eyes and watched how mist almost landed on its surface, and then fluttered away.

*Before more distractions come about, I must awaken Khat.*

*No threats have presented themselves. Yet the alluring sekhem that is present in everything around me, is overwhelming. Yet ritual can take place at ease, for the moment.*

I placed my back against the tree trunk, and shifted my from side to side to align my spine with its own. The tree's Akhu reached out for union in our breath. Its essence flowed into me as I rooted my seat into the fertile soft earth. A forgotten sensation of peace came over me.

*For too long, the stench of battle has been a close friend. And it has been ages since the sweet fragrance of nature has taken its place.*

The softened bark of this tree yielded a welcoming moisture that seemed to melt through my suit and into my battle-tethered skin. Suddenly, a creature ran across its surface and threw off my focus. It was then that I noticed the large variety of giant insects crawling over the tree.

Returning my focus to our unification, I was able to realign myself just in time to receive the projections of bark into my spine. Although slight discomfort made it difficult to stay still, I melded successfully.

Instantly, impressions of the season and weather patterns of this domain streamed through my consciousness. Also, because of its relationship with the insects, I gained the ability to perceive and store their life experience of this terrain in my body. From these things I got an inner-standing of this world and how to survive with them.

*The sekhem of their Ba flows through me, widening the pores of my skin to receive communication and sekhem.*

While this was taking place, a beetle the size of an adult cat, frantically shook its antenna in my direction—it seemed agitated and ready to attack. Yet the tree assured it, and the other insects on its bark, that I was no threat. Without pausing,the beetle turned its attention to a smaller insect, pierced its shell with its pincers then viciously devoured it in a matter of moments.

Through the connection, the impulse that set the cycles of endless vegetation and insects in motion spoke to my being. Their sekhem Shen Ra projected beautiful hues of greens and reds, that radiated from their centers deepening the grasp of the world around me.

*The awareness between my mind, flesh and akhu of the elder sister is like a first time occurrence of life.* My contact was taken in well, its intertwined skin, with mine, slowly absorbed my lower body and seat into its moist surface. An exhilarating sensation swept all my cells.

*Now for the HeKau. The sweet words of power.*

"Enuk wa Ka hna Ta Tn. Enuk wa Khat hna pet tn."

"Enuk wa Ka hna Ta Tn. Enuk wa Khat hna pet tn."

"Enuk wa Ka hna Ta Tn. Enuk wa Khat hna pet tn."

"Enuk wa Ka hna Ta Tn. Enuk wa Khat hna pet tn."

And yet as close as I was, I was still leagues away from its *essence.*

Everything I'd experienced was only on the surface. It was like having an open dialogue with a child and feeling the watchful eye of their mother—a mother who vehemently disapproved of her offspring's playmate...

*Let me close communication before I am drained, having to watch that eye is tiresome. Besides, I collected all the information I need...for the time being.*

It was fortunate that the sekhem content of this world was rich and raw, my minor cuts and bruises would heal rapidly.

*Now on to the real task at hand. Awakening Khat.*

"KhaT E Eu Nkht N Sekhmet N Ka."

"Khat E Eu Jser N Ra N Ka."

"Khat E Eu Nkht N Sekhmet N Ka."

"Khat E Eu Jser N Ra N Ka."

I was conscious of my body's mind and it was conscious of me. The web of our communication and connection pulsated about each another seamlessly.

"Khat? Khat do you *hear?* Time to awaken."

A deep sonorous voice answered. *"Once again you wake me from my slumber Neith, you must be in another bind with the Khemenu Nebu. Or another land, that you wish to dominate."*

"Yes, another land, except I am not so fixed on domination."

*"This place will be challenging, even for me, I needed to be able focus on the collection of cosmic energy about me. While you focus on funneling*

*and fine-tuning that energy into combative strength…and not a moment too soon!"*

"Khat, I know you sense that an aura is near us!"

*"Yes, something is near us."*

"I *hunger."* A ravenous voice spoke out from an unknown place—with savage intent.

Who and what was speaking? It was as if the air itself was alive with a flesh being's consciousness!

"You are not from here and yet I will *eat* you! I will become stronger eating your flesh! Your flesh that has mixed with the mind of this world!"

*I must get to my feet quickly!* I painfully ripped myself away from the tree and its bark that innervated my spine. My back momentarily bled before healing rapidly.

I sniffed the air. *Smells like an animal. Yes, it is an animal with heavy musk. A male creature.*

The weight and approach of it through the plant-life and over the ground was like a predator— its movement confident. Many kills were on its hide...it approached slow and steady, not wasting a step before it sprinted.

*"CHARGE* at *me!"* I shouted. "I want to know what fighting potential this world has!"

"Yes, sister, I am *coming."* The animal growled. "Your

experience on other worlds will not be sufficient for this one! Small one, your thriving essence will be *mine!*"

*It senses my combat ability on my aura shells!* I could feel this creature literally sniffing the accumulated Ka and Akhu essences on my aura, from my past battles on different realms.Every inhale it took drew in the information of those moments.

*But, there has never been an animal that I fell victim to, and I will not fall on this day.*

"That would be true if you were dealing with mere animals!" the beast growled.

*It can* hear *my thoughts?*

*It said 'animals.' I only feel one.*

*Wait.*

*Where did it go?*

I'd lost the physical impressions it was making on the air streams and the ground. The saliva had ceased to drop from its lips onto the leaves, and its heavy musk left the air…It was here in front of me but I could not see it...!

My sight could not pick it up, all I saw was a glob of dark energy.

*Khat?*

*"Pivot. Double arm block, cover heart, stick to limb. Feel its structure, pinpoint vital areas, find center of its body."*

# N

Had Khat moved a moment later, my heart would've been stuck to the end of its claws, while I ran the tongue of my mind.

It growled again. "Yes, sister fight *me!* Your life liquid will pump strongly in me and rouse the essence of this world!"

The beast's words shook the air about us. "Your flesh will become sweeter!" it whispered on the wind.

Despite my evasion, the impact of his first swipe smashed ferociously into my defensive stance and shook my insides fiercely. That attack was used only to bridge the gap and judge my response.

Now that I was in close quarters with it, it tried to change its position to be able to strike easier with its long arms. Yet, now that it was closer to me...I was able to see it.

Khat took over. *"Locate elbow, drop body weight into joint, as head comes down lunge with tight thumb into throat, pinch wind pipe and rip it out."*

It roared, then gurgled—still trying to claw at me while it choked on its own blood. Its dislocated limb plowed through the tree trunk when it missed me.

Jumping onto shoulder, I reached for sharp piece of broken wood. I clutched the wood tightly with both hands, squatted down and drove it into base of the leftside of his neck.

"ARRRGHHH!"

The ear-spliting agonizing cry of its final breath sent creatures flying away from their branches in their haste to escape. Apparently, this creature still possessed tremendous will power even as its life essence poured from its body.

Puncturing the heart was the only way to defeat and silence it. Aggressive strength was not enough, its structure was too heavy to strike at without using my full mass— much heavier than it looked.

Not only that, Khat found it difficult to access its full strength. Yet, my opponent had no difficulty freely expressing its might— much more than its ability should naturally shoulder.

His force was awesome! When I ripped out his throat, the flesh of the interior of his throat felt tensed and filled with small spikes. *Very* sharp.

*It has a natural defense mechanism. What kind of environment would create a beast that needed to protect his internal parts—even inside its mouth?*

Khat and I were one again. "*Drop immediately. Suck out poison. Grab that leaf over there. Chew it, mix it with your saliva. Spit it on your wounds and rub until the tingling is gone.*"

Surprisingly as the spirit of the beast left his vessel, he made one final attempt on my life. The poison secreted by those spikes was enough to force *my* Ka out of this body.

*Ha! That's a humorous thing to even ponder, for my body and I have been together so long through Esfet, Ma'at and beyond— what could tear us apart? But I almost went to the Duat by not paying attention.*

The Khemenu Nebu were so tired of my presence in the in-between world. Yet it was my constant visitation to that world that helped me develop my body.

*Sniff. The wind is becoming thick and unwelcoming, as if in response to my fresh kill. Strange. Well, there is no time to pursue any inquiry, I may stay on the move and find a secure position—along with nourishment.*

As I calmed down from battle, I took notice of how the supple soil was so welcoming to my battle conditioned soles. Each step was a long-awaited comfort to my feet— feet that had tasted many battle-fields and run so many leagues.

I was almost drawn back to my early years...as a young child in my mother's arms. We would walk through the hills of the village together, hand in hand, laughing at how the grass would tickle our toes as we brushed over the blades...

*So long ago. Another me.*

*Water... I can hear a brook up ahead, good. I can scrub the dried beast blood from my limbs, and remove the stench of its corpse from my being. I don't want to attract any others from its pack.*

*Almost there.* I could see in my mind's eye the water flowing off the stones and smell the currency building from its mist.

Why was it becoming so difficult to move through the small vines and plants? Were they reaching out for my ankles?

The closer I got the more they stuck out their thorns and entangled my feet. "That space of water is not for you…" Once again, strange communication of a being using the air for its words.

"Go away from here! Go bathe where your kind do! Not *here.*"

"How rude!" I said outloud. "There is no place in nature where I have been refused! I am a principle of nature itself. Sting my legs as much as you want. They have trekked through countless environments in harsh and pleasant conditions alike without complaint—"

*"Turn from here. This body of water will not welcome us. There are things in it, best avoided."* Khat warned.

And I listened to the heeding without hesitation. Doing so will continue the length of all these years of survival. Numerous years without ending, without rest.

Still there was a never a battle we hesitated to enter—

whether by force or choice.

My sense of warriorship always felt annoyed that some conflicts were better left alone.

When I changed my direction the plant-life became less aggressive. In fact, they seem to be laying out in a pattern. As I neared them, they folded together in a certain direction. I stopped, and they all stood straight and slightly flittered about in unison.

"Which way do you want me to go?"

They leaned to the right. A familiar scent was in the air as I went further in the direction I was being led.

Once again the air spoke. "Yes, you know this scent. Think. It is of beings like yourself. The self-aware thinking animal."

True, this was the scent of beings like myself. A fully grown one, somewhat like myself, and a smaller version of it. A mother and a daughter.

The light of a small house not far from here glimmered in the distance.

"You need rest." The plants thorns re-stimulated the earlier traces of poison, with their mild toxins, to make me stop.

"Why didn't you alert me sooner.? These toxins were hidden from my detection. I need more time to get information of this area..."

"Fine! This tree looks good enough for me to unite with—it seems almost familiar..." A piece of fruit just dropped in my lap from one of the branches.

"Eat stranger. Keep up your energy," spoke the tree.

*"Yes eat,"* Khat said. *"This tree is friendly and fruit is pure. Eat."*

The surface of this fruit was soft and rubbery, yet the taste is sour. *Mmmm. Delicious and full of energy. It's like I can taste the entire planet's life-force with each bite.*

"JUST BECAUSE SOME OF MY CHILDREN FAVOR YOU, PLEASE DO REMEMBER THAT YOU ARE PREY AND AN INVADER OF MY BODY."

This voice was *not* on the air, it was coming from all things around me. The presence is the same *mother* force that I experienced earlier.

*Listen to me: I am sure that you can hear my contemplations. So, you decided to address me directly instead of throwing your weight around though others. It's becoming clear to me, as moments pass, how I am perceived here.*

*However I have no intention of becoming fuel for your body's energy cycle. Now leave me as I shut my eyes and rest united with your child, surely you will not hunt or kill your own. Leave me be for the time being...oh sour one.*

I discontinued speaking to it with my mind— expecting no answer—and made my way back to the elder sister to reconnect with her.

## *Chapter Shemet*
## *The Hold*

Dvln got on my nerves as he paced back and forth and dragged his feet across the bar floor. But who can blame him—he has only a few more days before the All Nature claims him.

He should have left his family a long time ago. Maybe then his hands would not have been stained with their blood. Now his only solace is his son—the sole survivor— and his son's ability to complete the job I, Drrn, gave him.

"Dvln, have another drink and quit your fidgeting about! It bothers me...it's making me hot."

He stopped in his tracks when I finished my words, and pulled himself up on a barstool and ordered a round. *Poor guy. I guess the sight of what happened last time I got hot, is permanently etched in his tortured mind.*

My hands will never be clean again.

Nor will I have her to take away my pain.

"Dvln, you want a round as well?"

Dvln walked over to me holding a mug. He placed it down in front of me on the table and nervously withdrew his arm...thinking I wouldn't notice. It wasn't his usual nervousness either.

"Instead of trying to kill me, why don't you just wait for your son to return?" I said, trying to settle his irrational behavior—and to remind him exactly who was the alpha in this room.

*I know he tends to forget that because of our difference in the social scale—a scale that we, and others like us, have left long ago.*

*But is Dvln really this foolish? Did he think that the individual scents of the patrons mixed with the strong aroma of liquor would mask it?*

At least he could have used common sense and got it off his fingertips before passing me the mug.

"Suck your fingers!" I ordered.

He was almost paralyzed with fear, as he brought his right hand up to his mouth.

"No. Your other hand."

He shook and nearly urinated on himself.

"In fact...Shl, come here." I motioned for Shl to come over to us.

# N

Dvln had been involved with Shl for quite some time now. They met here in the bar that dreadful night, when he came bursting through its doors with blood soaked arms: holding an unharmed infant.

Shl was the only one who offered help, having her own experience in matters like this with her late husband. She'd helped him through his deep depression—after the murdering of his family— and even raised his son like one of her own.

Dvln shuddered from what he thought would happen next.

"Shl, would you be a dear and show your lover here some affection by kissing his fingertips."

"That's freaky. Where do you come up with this garbage...?" she said, lookin offended.

"But nothing is too much for my man." Shl took his hand by the palm and leaned in opening her mouth.

Dvln tried to move to stop her, but my glare froze him in his tracks.

Shl not only kissed her man's hand, she took all his fingers into her mouth and slowly licked each one. When she was done she kissed the top of his hand and walked off smiling.

Then she hit the floor face first.

*"Uh...Uh!"* his lips trembled in anxiety from what might happen to him next. Tears came running down his face as he

searched for the words to save his life.

There were none to be found.

No one in the bar moved to check on Shl...no one would dare without a word from me.

*This is bothersome—makes me want to stop giving and carrying out threats to my men when they challenge me.*

*Today, all I wanted to do was to relax in this chair, with these dim lights over me and the woody smell of the bar...*

*Sit here and watch the rain strike lightly against the windows, and imagine my pain washing away... like the dirt on their glass surface.*

Now all that had been interrupted, by someone who knew first hand the effects of The Fever. Someone who knew our plight intimately. We men, who have fallen out of favor with the All Nature for our deeds, deeds that are carved into our hearts—screaming to be released.

"I am going to give you two choices," my words broke the silence between me and Dvln.

His heart beat erractically in his chest, practically calling forth the violence from my body.

"W-w-what is it?" Dvln asked fearfully.

"Die fast and silently before your son comes."

"O-o-r?" He whimpered.

"Let him see you for a few more days after you complete

one mission."

"You want me to kidnap her? By myself?"

"Yes"

*Rkhm is near and he failed. I could sense it before he entered.*

"I choose the mission" Dvln whispered to me, with a pleading look on his face.

*He wants to keep it from his son.*

"Dad" Rkm called out soberly to Dvln. "I-I-I..." Rkm mumbled. Something or someone had scared him out of his wits.

"I know son. Go get cleaned up" Dvln spoke warmly to console him, and dismiss him at the same time.

He wanted to get him out of my sight, *and* out of the sight of his slowly dying step-mother who lay on the floor. Yet, there was another reason he wanted him out the room.

"But Dad I need—"

"I said *go!*" Dvln shouted.

I sniffed the air. *A fresh cut.*

"Come here Rkm" I said quietly, so as not to startle the boy, and at the same time keep him in the room.

Dvln tried to grab Rkm, and take him upstairs to his room, but Rkm had already made eye contact with me. He knew better than to ignore me. So, brushing his father aside was his best move.

Dvln reluctantly let go, allowing his arm to fall across Rkm's body. His attempt to create a boundary only made Rkm more nervous.

"Sit down" I gestured to the seat in front of me.

"Yes S-s-ir" Rkm timidly took a seat in front of me.

"Let me see it"

"See what?"

My smack nearly took his head off. And I'm sure the bouncing of his head off the tabletop re-adjusted his thoughts.

"Here..." he extended his arm while rubbing his jaw with his other hand.

A few patrons cleared out, as soon as the sound of soft flesh being bruised filled the room. Dvln stumbled to the bar and helped himself to the drinks they left on the counter. I guess it was the only thing he could do to console himself.

I checked Rkm's arm, and saw that the minor cut was made by the very blade given to him.

This young pup barely knew how to fuse the raw potential power of The Fever, and the natural ability from the All Nature—much less wield a blade.

Why had his father given him that thing? Did he want to increase his exposure to The Fever... So that he wouldn't be alone with his fate?

*Selfish. All of us are here.*

*There's something interesting about this cut though. It's fresh, mostly healed except for one area.*

I brought his arm closer, to focus my vision properly to magnify it. Rkm seemed more than frazzled by what happened with his failed mission.

Was this the same scruffy boy that forced his way into the bar a few days ago, demanding to be a part of the clan? So much bravado—even after he was told that he needed to spill blood until it was *cold* in order to join us.

I knew right away that he was infected by The Fever. But it hadn't taken a strong hold on his body...yet.

There was a faint scent of metal—metal that seemed to be moving about on his skin. As I looked further, I now saw what it was about the cut that he felt and interpreted as pain.

Microscopic red prawn-like creatures crawled about, withdrawing what looked like impurities from his body through the cut. I couldn't tell if they were red from being soaked in blood, or if it was their metallic shells.

Gradually his wound was being stitched up by a small group of them, while the others continued their mining of the toxins. I couldn't focus my eyesight any further, without getting a splitting headache from straining my eyes.

Yet, by the look of what they carried in their tiny apendages, it was something that definitely hindered the body.

The Fever.

They worked in a harmonic precision removing and mending. The stitching of skin and tissue along with the extraction of toxins from his bloodstream caused him to flinch every few moments.

"Rkm, how does your arm feel?"

My question shocked him out of his panic and worry—his fear of the consequences of failing a mission.

"It burns like my skin was frozen."

"Anything else?"

"It feels like fresh cool air is being passed over it."

"Anywhere else?"

"In my chest when I breathe...and anytime I think about fighting."

*Those things are all through his system, in every area where the early manifestations of The Fever took refuge. I am sure of it. They're cleansing his system and replacing damaged tissue.*

*I wonder...* "Rkm, you're in." I said nonchalantly.

Dvln sprang up in shock at my words.

"Yeah. You're now one of us." I patted him on the back.

"They'll be plenty of opportunities to make up for your failure."

Rkm relaxed his contenance and dropped his tense shoulders. He brought his arms to the table and rested his head on it. I looked sharply at Dvln, who attempted to conceal his pride, then I brought my attention to my mug of ale.

I intently looked at its frothing brim, then at Rkm, making sure Dvln noticed me. Dvln started to move towards us, tripping over the stools in the process. His motion was clumsy.

It was obvious that his mind was struggling between love for his son and the threat of me.

"Rkm, have a drink." I pushed the mug to him, while keeping a watchful eye on Dvln.

Dvln stopped, afraid to move forward an inch more. He stood still and helplessly watched...

First he glanced at Shl, sprawled out on the floor and twitching, then at Rkm and back at Shl.

Rkm was pulled out of his oblivion when he followed his father's eyes to Shl. He shrieked, and fell back in his chair, and clutched his chest. Wheezing and out of control, he shook and whimpered.

Rkm looked up at me during his performance, then straightened up amazingly fast. I guess my earlier open-hand slap, still stung enough to remind of his common sense.

One shouldn't act up in front of me—no matter what—I'm triggered easily by such behavior.

I think his blatant fear of a beat-down and those insect creatures must have relaxed his nervous system, so that his lungs would re-open.

"Shl...your mother is alright," I soothed. "Let her rest right where she is...Have a drink."

"B-b-ut" He said with quivering lips.

He tried to get up, so I pushed the mug slightly and sent some of the ale splashing on his lap.

"I said *drink*. You can wake her later."

And I meant what I said. *If my guess was right, Rkm may be saving two lives...that is, if he was still breathing after a few sips.*

Rkm nervously brought the mug to his lips and drank.

His father turned his back to us, not having the strength to bare the sight of his son's death.

At least, that's what coursed through his thoughts—thoughts that throbbed all about his body, in sync with the jack hammering of his heart.

All this I felt from my seat, and all this I ignored. Dvln trembled in his seat while drinking more of the lagers left by the patrons.

Rkm continued his own drinking, head tilted back as he

gulped steadily. His demeanor changed, as more and more of the ale dripped down his neck.

He slammed the mug down and stared me directly in the eyes. Even in this dimlit room, I can see his spirit blaze in his eyes.

"I'm *in*—right?" he said exhuberlantly.

"Wait..." I folded my hands, rubbed my knuckles on the hair of my chin.

*Something is going to happen.*

Just as Rkm opened his mouth to answer, he convulsed then reached out for me. He screamed until his voice was near hoarse and clutched at his stomach.

*"Stop!* Sit right there and quit your yelling! If you disobey, I will rip out your throat!" I said with agitation.

Rkm was in pain—but not so far gone that he wasn't still afriad of me. He moved restlessly in his chair, clutched at the sides of it and gritted his teeth.

Heavy sweat poured from his brow and then...

It was over.

He looked up and wiped his forehead and puffed wearily. "I don't know what happened...One moment I thought I was going to die and the next I felt like a new man."

*Those tiny creatures saved him. Not only are they ridding his body of*

*The Fever, they also attack any foreign may that might cause harm.*

*That attack that he had, just now, was the result of the war of those creatures against the poison meant for me.*

*I know this work all too well.*

"Dvln...pick up Shl and bring her here."

When Rkm saw his father drag over Shl, his poked out chest sunk in, immediately followed by his chin. Normally Dvln would have been able to sling her body over his shoulder with ease. But his strength was sapped, he'd allowed grief to enter his blood and muscles.

Rkm's eyes did not leave his mother and father as they approached. He stayed fixated on them, as he somberly pulled over a chair for Shl.

Dvln came over with his lover's limp body, lazily dropping Shl into the chair. A faint whisper of breath left her mouth, as she collapsed into the seat.

"Dvln, open her mouth." My words must have sounded as cold as ice to him and his son.

Yet, I know that my time soon approaches and that my cold disposition is the only thing keeping The Fever at bay.

While looking down at the table, Dvln grabbed Shl by the mouth and pried it open. His humanity seemed to have returned to him for a brief moment, when he ran his fingers down the side of face before letting go.

I pushed my chair closer to her, and saw by the lack of hue in her face that the poison had entered every cell of her body. It had spread quickly through her vessels leaving the skin raised with reddish-purple branch-like tracks—marring her dark ebony tone.

"Come over here, Rkm"

He got up from his chair still filled with confidence despite being shaken earlier. I grabbed him by the arm and ran my sharp nails across his skin.

I ignored his screams of agony, held his leaking arm over her mouth and wrung out larger drops of blood into it.

Dvln drew back horrified. "Let him go...let him go!" He pleaded with me, yet kept his distance.

"Shut up and massage her throat or something so she doesn't choke." My words shook him out of his frenzy.

"But she is *dead,*" he said grimly

Rkm started to struggle, attempting to break my hold. As his life-fluids splattered all over his clothes, the whole affair grew messy. I disgustedly threw him to the damp wood floor before he bled on my clothes as well.

*Another henchman that I'll have to support rather than him supporting me. Shit.*

## N

Rkm scrambled and slid back across the floor trying to get away from me—literally moving nowhere from being paralyzed in fright.

But I wasn't looking to chase him, my attention was on Shl. The whimpering and cursing of both father and son began to diminish into the background, as the pumping of Shl's heart embraced my focus.

The rate and strength of its pounding filled my ears...And then she coughed, spitting up the excess blood from her stomach.

How was I to know what the correct amount was, anyway? I'm sure that Rkm would have given me more trouble, if I'd asked to cut his arm and squeeze some into a glass for his mother to drink. A lot more trouble.

Shl's skin gradually returned to its normal beautiful ebony tone, and her breathing normalized.

I turned away from them and their family reunion to watch the rain. The drops striking against the windows glass seemed to wash away more of the dirt...

## *Chapter Fedu*
## *Words*

Mere flesh creature—yes, *you*—reading this book entitled *N,* please excuse me for not introducing myself earlier.

I am known as *Khusat,* which would be the closest approximation of what you know as a name.

Yet, if my true essence were to be uttered your slime-like frame would not be able to endure it, and you would most likely perish.

For lack of better expression, I am what you would call a *planet.*

Although you may not be able to imagine that it is possible for a being such as I to communicate with you, here I am speaking directly to your consciousness through these pages.

Doubtful? Is it so hard to grasp that I may have a consciousness and ability to convey feeling and intent intelligently. Are you so far gone and removed from your true nature, that you have forgotten universal truth?

Nevertheless, it is fortunate that you are reading this book—that you have acquired by whatever means you have. To think that your feeble fingers will flip through these pages with mindless fervour, in an attempt to satisfy your chase for pleasure alone!

You, the reader, who is now moving with my sister may gain benefits from the occurrences which are about to unfold in these pages.

The Great Year of my sister's house, which is taking place now, according to your time, has already passed, and brought some of your kind here—to my body.

Where I was once only populated by plantlife and animals alone, I soon became filled by your kind. Humans. Lelu Amelu. Remetyu. Or whatever other title you managed to give yourself.

Of course, in order for humans to survive on my surface, I needed to enhance their genetic structure. It wasn't the easiest process, since most of them simply re-materialized from their original forms—rather than going through the birthing process.

The majority of them had no memories of their prior lives. Still they experienced anguish, when I caused their melanin and carbon levels to rise dramatically—increased their fortitude to survive and their synergy with me.

But, I will not go into depth with their story. I will tell you of the mighty entity which has just invaded my body. One who thinks that she will have dominion over it.

I will let her think for the time being, that all her thoughts and experiences are her's alone. She may express herself freely. Yet, all my sisters' and brothers' worlds know that she is mine to do with as I wish, according to the laws...just like the rest of these crawling things upon my surface.

This foreign being has yet to fully grasp that everything on this world is mine—for I *am* this world.

Those of you who did not survive my sister's transformation, will not do to me what *they* did to her.

Your selfish pursuits for power and pleasure—*human* pursuits—without any inkling of how to respond with generosity, became the instrument for my sister's suffering.

I will not tolerate the tunneling, the scraping, the burning, the yelling and the engulfing defecations that spread across her magnificent skin, followed by piercing into her vibrant womb.

Regardless of the atrocities, she still loved her children. When that great time came in her home, all her brothers and sisters gathered to show her respect and rejoice in her change as she moved through the seven sister's house. Many beings on her surface were not destined to stay with her.

So their essences came here with me: her sister. Or should

I say it in a way, so that yours and the other finite minds reading this may comprehend?

She mourned her offspring and pleaded with me to watch over them. It was only her everlasting love that convinced me to agree to her request. Although what your kind has done to her was pre-destined in the cycle of things, I still find it difficult to accept.

Yet, the one called *Neith*, is not of this family. She rejected your mother planet— my sister—millennia ago in pursuit of battle.

And I will tell you this: Neith's stay here will not be pleasant. And she is only avoiding my direct hand passing over her because of her relationship with the All Parent.

So, I will remove her by her own accord. This family that she approaches may not be as hospitible as she may think them to be.

But regardless of the fact that they are not as easily influenced by me, as their wilder cousins (what you may call animals, whose primal instinct dominates their being) they are still mine.

My children.

I will not make it easy for Neith.

And I will find a way to separate her essence from her

body.

# N

N

## *Chapter Shemet*
## *Efforts*

While passively eyeing our new 'Focal Tkkn' in the living room, I asked Mother the same as I always do in the shadow hours.

"Mother the meal is almost done, should I bring down the fire?"

"Yes beloved. You need not ask me what you already know." She responded in the same manner as she always does, knowing exactly what I was about to do.

Without a pause she continued to set our table— our bowls meticulously placed to catch the energy flow from the window. No waste of movement or effort entered her ritual.

While she was occupied, I removed the red hot coals with my hand and placed them carefully in the sandbox for latter use.

As I put the last of them in the box, I heard what I expected to hear.

# N

"Jnfr, how many times must I tell you not to do it that way. It's too careless."

"Mother, the other way takes up too much time. It's annoying."

*"Jnfr!"* she raised her voice and the things unbolted to the floor were almost shaken apart.

Long ago I refurnished the house with materials made from the strongest elements within our wooded area... And sometimes I feel the only result was my chiseled muscular tone, not the preservation of our furniture.

"You know we cannot risk crushing anymore coals.They are too difficult to locate, even those peoples who are closest to the All Nature are not always so fortunate," she finished.

Mother always spoke with the clear cut reasoning that was never to be challenged. Sometimes her repressed feelings hit the house like a hurricane. So it was no wonder that our current rustic and homely-look suited our living behaviors.

"Not one got crushed as I removed them from the pit. Can't you smell the meal's flavor clearly without a hint of ash?" I asked almost challengingly—knowing full well the consequences.

*This free spirit of mine is so predictable.*

She walked over to me just as I removed the last coal. Just

when my hand passed over the pot, she smiled and pushed her palm into my abdomen. My natural response was to bend over at the hip which knocked a bit of ash from the coal.

Her smile gradually went to a slight show of teeth, which meant I was in for a lesson if any of that ash fell into the pot. I swung my opposite arm over the pot and caught the ash in between my fingertips.

I returned my mother's earlier smile with one of my own and flicked the ash in the sandbox after placing down the coal.

"You know what? There is not a trace of ash, just like you said." She replied smugly as if plotting something.

"The aroma is actually sweeter than the last meal we had. It would be nice if the house was cool this evening.
Jnfr—"

Before she could continue, I gathered up the tools needed to cool the house.

*Ah... Mother knows very well that those ten minute sprints up the snowy mountain irritate me. She always has cool evenings. Oh well, let me gather up my snow boots and Ice-Cutter...*

I looked back as I left out the door, and saw her smirking. *Oh mother!* I giggled to myself. She *always* has cool evenings.

## *Chapter Sesu*
## *Sa Sekhmet*

He had five left from the nine he'd started with. Four of the finely crafted daggers were sunk into the throats of the foreign creatures—these men with metal head coverings and fire sticks.

*And I, Apep, greedily watch.*

*The essence steaming off their bodies is not as appealing, as the prey who has now become their predator.*

*Sa Sekhmet is the name his heart uttered from its first beat beating...Rather intriguing that this dark olive man of small stature, possesses such a strong fighting spirit and physical prowess.*

*Yessssh, his valiant effort against these foreign invaders will ensure that my young will have full bellies in the shadow hours.*

*SSSSSSSssssss...one man such as he will rip*
*his own body to shreds, to defeat a group of four and twenty men. His flesh will heave the cosmic force of battle.*

Before Sa Sekhmet could retrieve one of his weapons, he heard footsteps attempting to muffle their advance. He darted quickly from out their vision.

He sought to take refuge in one of the jagged-edged barked trees. Despite the trees barbed hide digging into his inner thighs, his face remained stoic...as he made his ascent into its high branches.

He tightly coiled himself around the first limb he made contact with. Sa Sekhmet bit into his pinky finger, to stave off the painful irritation caused from the sap that got into his cuts.

Had he time to feel the tree, he would have known about the saps poison— the tree's natural defense. Even though he was in pain, a smile stretched across his face.

He was excited.

*His heart begins to race—not with anxiety—no, with the blood of Sekhmet! I did not see this! It escaped my tongue's sight!*

*This man is not another mere lump of flesh with borrowed energy from the cosmos. He is the embodiment of cosmic principle itself!*

The foreign creatures below searched in vain for Sa Sekhmet, mostly due to their lack of natural intuition, while he slowly peeled off some of the bark of the branch and broke it into pieces the size of his cuts, which now widened to gashes.

He whispered a few words on to the pieces and then spat on them. Keeping balance in his position, he skillfully laid the strips on his wounds then spoke in a few more whispers.

The blood that was flowing out the gapes along with the dried parts began to absorb into the makeshift dressings.

As the blood was being pulled into the bark, it clutched

onto the ripped skin and dragged the skin along with it. Once these things ceased movement, the areas that were damaged were now replaced with bark-like skin.

Sa Sekhmet held a look of content on his face as he carefully reached for a dagger from his pack. He drew the dagger out, fixing his eyes on its bright gleam, and looked fiercely at it.

The surface reflected his energy on its face. He held it up to his lips.

"Seek the hard cobra," he uttered to the blade's surface.

*I see. He is trained in the Art of Mafdet as well— the attitude that treats the body parts of opponents as different manifestations of snakes.*

The foreigners began to spread out in four directions. One of the men doubled back towards his direction, this was an opportunity that calls for precise timing.

When Sa Sekhmet made his move, he knocked some leaves loose from their branches. The man heard the rustling sound and began to look up. But Sa Sekhmet had already flung the dagger up in the air with force and leapt to the next tree's branches.

When as the man extended his chin to the sky, the dagger that had been tumbling and gathering speed, plunged itself deep into his throat penetrating into his neck-bone.

# N

*"I have found the hard cobra..."* the blade whispered as it made his throat a sheath.

The man attempted to remove the dagger as soon as it hit its mark. But failed...he collapsed to the ground.

His comrades came running to his aide, some staying back to encircle the area. Sa Sekhmet positioned his body tightly around the branch and lay: silently poised. He slowly began to match the beat of his heart with the rhythm of the jungle.

He knew getting into the pattern of flow with the life forces around him, would give him the advantage against the foreigners.

The fragrance given off by the trees and plants began to change to a sour scent. The vegetation didn't like these beings that entered their domain, carrying malicious intent in their spirits.

Sa Sekhmet felt their anger, and sent back his scent to communicate his shared emotion.

He encouraged the surroundings to lend him their power.

Their essence.

It started with the vegetation. A misty vapor began to rise from their surfaces and flow towards him. His pores expanded, and sucked the energy into his body, his skin rippled like a pond.

He could feel his mother grow strong in him. Sekhmet's teeth clenched... then her jaw sprung open wide within his chest.

She let out a roar that echoed in the realm of the plants. They responded by stretching ever so slightly their leaves and branches to the direction of Pet and Ra...asking for their rays.

The animals stopped their grazing noticing the quality of their food changed and the universal vibe of The vegetation shifted from the defensive stance it had earlier on.

Once they determined what was happening, they shared in the issuing of strength to Sa Sekhmet. All animals, small and large, raised their limbs and sent their essence forward.

*I almost find myself joining in.*

*But that would shift the natural flow of things; for I, Apep, to participate in anything of this manner.*

The animals opened their hearts to Sa Sekhmet and he took from them what he needed.

The Ka of Sekhmet which lay deep in Sa Sekhmet's chest spoke: *"Nfr Sa. That is excellent my son. Take only what you need from the small creatures, so not to slow their escape from those that might eat them."*

*"Take all that you wish from the large ones, so they may work harder to catch meals."*

Sa Sekhmet savored the plant and animal force that flowed throughout his being. The plant inhabitants expressed need for Ma'at to be re-established.

And he was the tool for that need to be carried out. No longer would he move in stealth—now was the time to strike a mighty blow.

One by one he prepared his weapons. He opened his mouth and bit down on one of the dagger's handle. He fixed his Khepesh to the flat of his back, to make it accessible for finishing attacks then placed two daggers in his right hand and the last in his left.

*I feel exhilarated with the anxiety of finally seeing Sa's blood-thirst grow...run its course, and tear these men's bodies and spirits asunder.*

*As I sit crouched and coiled in the hollow bark*
*of this Babobab tree, my tongue catches the mist of these foreigners' sweat which has been steaming off their bodies these past moments.*

*Yessssssssshh—they will make fine meals indeed!*

*They have no idea how much of their life essences escape from their being, as they literally spew out their emotions with sickened hearts.*

*I will take all the bodies, that still possess some energy, to my young!*

Sa Sekhmet lept down to the man closest to the tree. As the man looked up, he spat the dagger out his mouth with the full power of his jaw and tongue.

Unlike before he did not whisper on to the blade. He did not need to. The blade remembered.

The dagger buried itself into the man's left eye. In mid-air, he whipped his left wrist sending a blade hurtling at another man rushing towards him.

The dagger tore through the man's chest, ripped his insides... then traveled out through his back to bury itself up to the center of the handle in another man behind him.

Just as Sa Sekhmet's toes touched the ground, he reached with his right hand out for the blade in the man's eye. The force of his landing drove it deeper into the man's head. The foreigner's legs gave way and he fell back hanging off the dagger.

Another came rushing, looking to take advantage of Sa sekhemet's position...

*Their battle rage blinds their senses, I can taste the current on my tongue, and it charges my Ka. Delightful!*

Sa Sekhmet gave no thought to letting go of the bone handle, whose blade was tightly lodged into the foreigner's skull. He stepped forward with his left foot and pivoted his right side from his hips.

As the momentum built, he tightly clutched the handle, and lifted his arm up and swung the now limp body hanging off it. The charging attacker sought to stop his motion and ended up tumbling into his dead companion.

His stumbling put stress on his knees—the bones that held them in place snapped and pushed through his skin. He collapsed on top of the body of his comrade, and was swept along with it until they both hit the side of a tree.

Sa Sekhmet instinctually let go of the dagger. Just then five men came rushing at him with their long swords drawn. He kept the motion of his spinning and tossed one of the daggers in his left to his right hand.

He crouched down, and as he came back around swung at the attackers' knees. They fell in a clumped mass of bodies onto the forest floor. He swung his Khepesh and finished them off in turn.

"Has she found them yet?" he whispered to himself. "HAVE YOU *FOUND* THEM YET? I tire of this meaningless killing!" he yelled.

"Although their transitions served as a distraction." Sa Sekhmet finished quietly.

A strange feline sound filled the air.

"Yes mother..." called out Sa Sekhmet.

The men ceased their attack and began to back off, although they still kept a watchful eye on him.

*They're confused as to whom he's speaking to. But I know.*

*I know very well.*

*He is speaking to Neith.*

*My young are dead by now and I could not foresee it because I was so focused on my prey.*

"Prepare yourself."

*Sa Sekhmet speaks in a quiet manner as he drew back the bush that covered my resting spot. Amongst all this riveting sweet chaos, I missed something about this one called Sa Sekhmet—something very important to my being.*

*And now, my tongue senses that with all the speed I possess, I will not be able to avoid— Saaaaa...!*

* * *

Once again, I've seen visions of this person called Sa Sekhmet fighting that accursed Apep!

*And still I don't know why!*

I've seen him through Apep's eyes, because of that foul serpent's deep bite and it's sekhem still coursing through my system to this day.

My journeying into that time, has yet to reveal the reason why I am seeing them. There is so much of my past that is completely blocked off from me—

*What was that?*

*I could have sworn someone just ran past me!*

The burst of their speed pulled a trail of leaves through the air behind them.

*Let me replay the image my eyes captured in slower motion...*

*Ah, I see.*

It was a large woman, at least eight feet tall, slender and youthful. There is a large pack on her back. She went in the direction of the mountain that towers over the enomorous trees of this forest.

*That confirms the presence of those beings I picked up on earlier.*

*Ugh! I am a bit unsettled. The effect of the journeying has taken a toll on my rational thought. Something seemed familiar about what was revealed to me.*

*I need to go back and retrieve that information, before mother finds a way to uproot me from her child...*

# N

## *Chapter Sefheku*
## *You Know*

I loved these moments in the mountains, even though I complained about them to mother every chance I got. She would never hear me admit that she knew her daughter, Neith, like the beat of her own heart.

Never.

*Will you look at that? The ice has reformed nicely from the last time I cut it. I love the way it glistens in the light of the twin moons.*

*Poetry.*

*This hard water against the soft luster pouring from the sky and I with my ice-cutter ready to hew it down, so that it may be born again.*

It beckoned to me and I would come to it... The way it yielded to my cut.

*Mmmmmm. Look at me talking about doing this work like it was some boy I am longing for!*

There was one I longed for and yet he was in the city— where the lights never seemed to dim. But nothing could compare to the lights out here in the woods, especially up on this mountain.

*The air is fresh and the clouds go on without end across the night sky. No time to daydream.*

*Its funny how I act like I do not like to come up here, and yet once I am here, I never want to leave.*

*Let's see...where should I cut this time? Right here at the base where it projects. Or here, while I think about things.*

*I am naive. Mother has been preparing me for something, discreetly training me all these years. I have*
*always known this.*

*Yet this is the first time I'm admitting it to myself.*

She especially acted peculiar when it came to Father— any mention of him made her a little on edge. I mean, he didn't leave us because he wanted to.

The Fever made him go.

No matter how much we cooled the house his body heat still rose. Not matter how many visits we made to the city for collective cures or the inner woods for natural herbs, the sweat still poured from his skin whenever he was around Mother and me.

Along with the sweat came the words...the hurtful words. The arguments with Mother took a toll on her good nature.

Even though she was still loving, there was a hidden feeling of sadness in her spirit. Maybe these constant trips were a way to hold onto a piece of him.

*I must focus my mind on my task.*

All movement must be a progressive climb to harnessing my essence with the All Nature.

*I slowly draw the ice cutter from its sheath, and breath out once it fully leaves the casing—raise it to the sky...*

*Notice how the blade reflects the moons in the night sky, along with the stars that spread across the dark blue.*

*Experience the energy from the surroundings soak into the blade. Take it in both hands holding the handle down, look out into the top of the trees. See how they gather in clusters across the horizon.*

*Their peaks appearing like the top of dark waves. Take in the night into my arms— the unseen strength and calm. My center at one as I hoist my cutter. Breath in. Cut...*

"YEEEEEEEEEEE—ARRRRRRR!"

A good sized piece slid off evenly. Yet sometimes I wondered why it always included so much ritual. I quickly secured it in the carriesr alongside the clear crystals so it wouldn't melt before I get back home.

The feeling in my back muscles and hips tightened to their maximum. I released and sent tingles in between my legs. My womb feels so powerful every time I cock back the ice-cutter and swing.

*You know when I think about it, mother is very shrewd. I can tell that she changes the straps on the carrier everyday—gradually forcing me to increase my balance and internal strength.*

As I made my way down the mountain I was reminded of my many trips up its face. The varying sizes of indentations in the ground, show that I'd been doing this since I was a small child...right after Father left.

Mother had always been so open about things, and yet there was something she is concealing. Something was definitely unusual in the air tonight for me to be—

"*Wake up. NOW.*" Khat's warning exploded in my consciousness. "*You're surrounded by wild animal, the pack of that one you sent to the next realm!*"

## *Chapter Khemenu*
## ***Wolves***

*"There are at least 13 of them— all heavy with bloodthirst—some in the trees, others in the brush!"*

I was ripped by Khat from the journeying of my memories so suddenly, my head was on fire! It was so difficult to get an accurate feel for their distance!

And they remained hidden from my sight! I could sense their presence, but not the impressions of their paws on the surface where they stood.

"You have taken our brother! Now we will take *you* for him!" threatening words carried on the wind. "Your flesh, as foreign as it is to our senses, we will devour!"

I could feel their hunger rising as a group, they would soon be upon me.

And I was just beginning to love the feeling of communicating with the nature around me!

Fine. I would make an example of the first one for the rest. *"Come*—come with all you've got!" I called to the edge of darkness before me.

"Delicious! Your will to survive is sending the most tempting flavor through you flesh!" More threats... yet this time the texture was different.

"Yes, this one will make a fine meal for us all! I want her liver!" Their taunts were quickly becoming annoying.

"You can have my fists!" I cried out to them from under the Elder Tree, and released my charged musk into the air.

The air shifted strongly and pushed violently against my body, one of them was rushing forward. Massive teeth and claws became visible only at the moment when its arm lashed out at me.

My heart remained steady. Khat moved within me: "*Rip branch. Shove sharp end in mouth as jaws open. Push until body drops. Keep top of head close to elbow. When head lowers, crack the back of the neck.*"

The beast's body now lay twitching next to me—heaving its last breaths from its huge chest. I pushed my body up over his mass to see what was coming next.

Nothing.

I only saw the huddled plants and trees collectively creating darkness in the distance. I relaxed my breath and allowed the impressions they made on the environment to be revealed.

The beasts were keeping their physical presence masked very well. The first one was sent to test my strength and response. It didn't expect me to react to its leap, while the rest were waiting.

My nostrils burned from the secretion of poison—Khat's poison— into the air. It was still fuming from my mouth. My attack did not take away from my positioning, although I was not in the most superior one.

They adjusted their positions and postures, changing them from the one their fallen kin had taken. And their group attitude affected the atmosphere: the vegetation began to wilt and turn black as the situation progressed.

*Adapative creatures.*

*Wait.*

*A force different from the others nearby... it is* human and familiar.

*"NNP!"* a strong feminine voice called out.

Then she strode out from the darkness of the woods and walked boldly toward us, brandishing a huge axe.

The aggressive sekhem of the beasts hid in refuge leaving no traces of any hostility across the area. Plants and trees turned green once more.

In an instant, the remaining numbers in the pack became visible and littered the area with the huge bodies. All appeared docile.

She towered over us with her long-limbs, that easily pushed aside the thick leaves of plants in her way. A simple one piece blue dress draped lightly over her body, accentuated her beautiful dark skin and athletic muscular tone.

*She is like me.*

*But why I didn't detect her until right before she spoke?*

"Nnp, leave her alone." She said, less aggressively.

"Jnfr! You are *not* a sight for sore eyes! What business is this of yours? Is this one yours? Is she your kin? Before you answer, I'll tell you that she *isn't*. If she were, we would not be here in front of her ready to tear at her flesh."

Their anger and hostility returned— instantly affecting everything around us, except for this giant and myself.

"She is... my pet." the giant female said with conviction.

*Pet? PET?*

The pack snarled and snickered at her remark, loosening their tensed muscles and decreasing the rapid pumping of blood by their hearts. The scent of their sweat changed— no longer giving off fear and aggression. Even the foliage, relaxed their stems and roots.

"Pet, huh?" The leader of the pack mocked in disbelief.

"Yes, pet! Would you *eat* a pet of mine? One that I love so dear?" she rebutted in a dominant tone, and almost playful innocence of a child.

"Why doesn't she carry your scent?" Their leader was not convinced. He inched up closer to me.

"Well, we have her wash everyday as you can see she is…abnormal. Who knows what germs she has?"

*Abnormal. So it had come down to this. Neith, the fear and bane of numerous worlds, a pet! How humiliating.*

Well, I must endure. I might not be able to extract the information needed from them, if I bashed everything in sight. I was drained too. If I continued this way, I would inadvertently draw upon the bloodthirsty venom of Apep.

This was bothersome.

"I wouldn't mind some more of your pack's powerful flesh tonight. Still, I do have a stew simmering at home right now," she said nonchanlantly.

"Now, now Jnfr." Their leader relaxed his stance recognizing he might have gone too far. "The All Nature has granted you your family's fill of our pack this month."

"Furthermore, the Cocoa Bushes you have planted are not

fully grown yet, so we have not been able to produce any more cubs without the juice from its barks," he said submissively. He turned to leave.

"Nnp, before you go, have one of your underlings fetch my pet something to eat." Jnfr commanded.

Nnp looked back at her fiercely, but Jnfr just smiled. In the midst of her smiling, psychic waves came off her body and struck Nnp *hard.*

He shook his head vigorously then turned to his pack, singling out what appeared to be the runt. "So be it! Keep your pet on a short lease!" snarled Nnp.

The pack took its leave, allowing me no physical signs of their departure. The gradual absence of stench was my only indication.

"So...pet. What do you think about our dogs?"

She was like a child—pushing her agenda without a formal greeting.

*Dogs? Those are dogs?* Well her stature was extraordinary for her age and then again, why would that be out the ordinary to me? How could someone like me set a bar?

I should be more interested in her deductive reasoning. She knew that I wasn't from here.

She scrutinized me closely, before placing her sack and axe

down on the ground, then taking a seat next me.

"Oh, here comes your meal"

One of the 'dogs' came back, shyly walking through the thick brush, carrying something in its mouth. He was a smaller version of the one I did away with, yet, larger than any full grown wolf I had ever seen.

He placed what looked like a rabbit at my feet and timidly pushed it to me with his nose. When Jnfr moved towards me, he nervously drew back then ran off.

Normally, I only eat flesh as a last option when I am drained and there is nothing else available. But a weakened state always makes it difficult to draw upon raw sekhem.

Presently, it would take a great deal more focus and effort to configure this planet's level of sekhem than it does to extract it from food. And since I am not fully acclimated to my surroundings to know what vegetation I can digest, or what steps are needed to restructure my biology, this flesh will have to due.

Jnfr drew a circle in the soil and placed the animal in the center. She crossed her legs and positioned herself in front of the circle, motioning for me to do the same.

"Hurry—while the spirit is still present!"

She reached her hands out for me and I took them into

mine my forearm was easily engulfed in her grasp.

"All Nature, we thank this being for its flesh and seek to make its energy useful in our activities. Please grant us the benefits of the best parts of it—the parts of it that sought to protect it, please give it to its future generations. Release it from its body so that it may travel back to you in peace."

The spirit of the animal slowly rose out from its limp corpse in a thick mist. It hopped around through the air and stopped in front of Jnfr: sniffing her out.

Jnfr smiled. "Please take your entrails with you friend and cleanse your blood." She spoke directly to it as it floated in the air in front of her. It rubbed its head against her hand, its misty form dissipating and re-forming in the process.

It timidly approached me and jerked back, sneezing and shaking vigorously.

*It must be offended by my presence... and the smell of the fresh-kill on my body.*

While moving over to its physical body, its hue began to glow a bright violet and became concentrated without dispersing energy from its core.

Suddenly, streams of energy shot out its being and pierced into the lifeless shell. They appeared like translucent tubes connecting the two forms together.

The spiritual body arched its back, came to stand on its hind legs and radiated an incandescent green. It tremored causing the shell on the ground to shift back and forth.

"Watch carefully. I am sure you have never seen a process like this before," said Jnfr proudly.

She was right. Although I have seen countless ways to purify the flesh for consumption, I have never seen a process such as this. I knew that in most cases the main goal has always been to preserve the Ra energy that was imbued into the cells.

As I kept a watchful eye over the ritual, my interest piqued when I saw what looked like organs travel through the tubes towards the Akhu. Then without a moment passing, the same tubes feed back into the body a greenish blue fluid.

The body glowed vibrantly for an instant, then settled down still leaving a noticeable exuberance.

The Akhu drowsly hopped back over to Jnfr, it seemed drained and desiring rest. Jnfr rubbed her nose to it and it breathed out some lifeforce into her nostrils.

As its exhaustion became more evident, it made its way down her arm and dropped something small from its mouth into her palm. It then leapt into the air, speeding pass the embrace of the enormous trees, then upon reaching the clearing burst into millions of particles.

Tiny snowflake like energy spheres fell from the sky and blanketed everything immediately around us, giving all that it touched a soft luminosity before dissipating.

"That is how we keep the meat fresh and pure. We ask the spirit to purify the body and re-vitalize the blood before it makes it departure," Jnfr explained, as she quickly skinned the animal, separated the flesh from bone and seasoned it before placing it in a pan from her pack.

She covered it securely with a lid and began other tasks. She remained quiet in her work, almost meditative, gathering enough twigs to start a cooking fire. She pulled out a slim crystal and pressed her thumb into a slight depression on its surface.

A thin beam of light shot out from its tip into the gathered wood and ignited a fire. Once the food was done, she divided it between us. We both gave our respects, then ate.

The food was so rich and filled with vitality, it literally melted in my mouth—carrying none of the usual heaviness flesh embodied.

As I hungrily tore into it, my eyes were captured by the night sky and its many stars. The comfort I experienced was astounding.

"You look tired. Exhausted. Sleep."

## N

*Why do I feel drowsy all of a sudden? Something about how she said "sleep" hit my skin and relaxed my muscles.*

*Khat, what is happen—?*

# N

N

# *Chapter Pasedju Per Voices*

"JNFR! Why did you bring her *home?* You should have left her where you found her!"

"Mother, she was in trouble! I knew that I had to help her!" Jnfr protested. "There was no part in me that could refuse. Despite the forces around her that made her repelling, I could not help what my heart felt."

"Look at her! LOOK!" her mother scolded while pointing at me. "She is not...not of this world. She is small and youthful, yet I can sense she is older that our elders by eons."

"Foreign. Stranger. The All Nature will not receive her well."

*Another reference to the All Nature again. Could that be the same entity that claims to be the planet? Jnfr apparently carried me to her home after I passed out— another mistake on my part.*

*I'm letting my guard grow too lax, to let myself black-out in the presence of a potential threat. But I guess a pet cannot be expected to do any less.*

*How did she knock me out with only a word? And why didn't Khat respond?*

*Was it the meal?*

The mother spoke harshly to Jnfr, yet projected none of that energy towards me. She was much larger than her daughter, and neither of them displayed any signs of backing off. The two giants stood face-to-face only, separated by the large floor table between them.

The evening light from the twin moons shone through their wide windows and blanketed their massive frames. Rapid hand gestures, and the swaying of their upper bodies against the light, gave the appearance of dancing moonbeams as their figures cut in and out of them.

This was a power struggle between the experienced and the virtuous. They paid me no attention once they began to argue—which was as soon as I came through the door.

*I must say, their floor cushions are very comfortable and appear to be made of animal hides and buckwheat hull filing.*

*I'm glad to be calm in unknown circumstances.*

*My life is one long unknown circumstance.*

The interior structure of the house appeared to be constructed from smoothed out timber. Every piece I looked at, was a statement of focused and spiritually devoted work.

*In their minds, high ceilings that are proportional to their bodies are average. Yet for me it's like being in an temple.*

The dark black floorboards seem to be stained by a mixture of sap, flower essences, earth and other elements found in trees, and even the marrow of animals.

The synergy of these things produced a rich ebony hue. In every corner large illuminated, white quartz pillars were surrounded by Djed-like pile batteries. They were the power source.

And the house was well-lit and soothing to the eyes. Sliding doors constructed of long-hanging bamboo separated the majority of the rooms. From the looks of things, there were no man-made constructions that were wasteful of nature's resources. The only metals used were for kitchen utensils and equipment to harness or collect raw materials.

From the looks of it, I was in the family room. To the center, there was a round seated area built into the floor with more animal hide cushions encircling it.

A large onyx crystal hung from the ceiling into the center

of this area. The crystal extended through the roof. Possibly an antennae. There was also some artwork around the circumference of it similar to Medu Ntcher.

I sniffed the air. I'd just remembered how famished I was. Even though the purified meat from earlier sustained me, it was only for that moment.

*I need more. My body requires much—especially after traveling the distance I have, and smashing into the earth.*

"Now she expects us to feed her." Jnrf's mother signed with resignation. "Well, what do they call you?" She looked down at me expectantly.

"Neith," I replied amicably.

"Nth?" My name left her lips differently.

*They appear to utter personal names without much use of vowels. I can remember doing the same as a child.*

"Yes, Nth," I answered in her tongue.

"Curious name. Not surprising though, since you do not come from this world."

"And how do you know that?" I waited to see what information she'd share.

"Your smell is funny. And your body propotions are too small for your age. Your weight is too light."

*Her perception is powerful.*

"And...you fell from the sky—we saw it open up, we *felt* the air shift as it never did before," she explained while relaxing her stance.

"All of the animals have been acting peculiar since you hit," she went on. "You are a foreigner—a stranger to this world. The All Nature does not totally embrace you. I can see how some of its essence is even repelled by you." The Mother commented while she walked around me, and inspected me from a distance.

"Jnfr, didn't you see that around her?"

"Yes, a little...What stood out most was the scent of blood on her flesh from a wild beast and her bloodthirst," Jnfr answered.

Her mother nodded. "Quite a lot for someone of her stature, wouldn't you think?"

*Bloodthirst? Well I guess I haven't matured as much I thought.*

"Jnfr, secure the ice. I will attend to our guest and her bloody swimsuit. Toss out those cushions as well. She's made quite a mess of them."

Her attitude had changed drastically, and her voice lost most of its petulance.

"So Nth, let me bathe you and get your things cleaned."

"I am very grateful for your kindness. What is your name?"

"Tzwk..." She gestured with her hand,"This way please," and lead me to a descending staircase hidden behind a sliding door panel.

On the panel, there was a watercolor painting of a waterfall, the depth of it brought out the painter's emotion. It was undying love.

As I walked down the short staircase behind Tzwk, I could feel the passion and loyalty of that love in her movements. She looked to me, as I walked off the last step. Her eyes were deep and piercing.

"I am fine, Nth. A man can sometimes leave a scar... that we do not want to forget."

And with that, she walked through two large black cotton flaps into another room. I followed behind and lifted up the flaps rather than pushing through them. But I couldn't afford to leave my guard totally down.

My body was gently hit with a heavy mist and my nostrils widened taking in the fragrance of peppermint... or at least that was it smelled close to.

Whatever first struck my eyesight, I took a few mental pictures of. Gradually the interior of the interior of the room became visible. Dim soft lighting provided by the corner crystals, gives it a warm atmosphere.

To both sides of the room, sat stones piled up on a grating over a low-lit fire. Next to these were wooden buckets of water and a long wooden ladle.

To the back of the room, close to the wall, a pool the size of a pond lay built into the floor surrounded by colored stones of different sizes. In front of this, was a long wooden table with open spaces along its surface.

During my intake of this simple beauty, Tzwk appeared from behind a screen, which was next to the entrance.

I didn't sense when she moved from me, that irritated me...more than a bit. She had in her hands, towels, a water bucket and other materials.

She gracefully walked over to the table, and knelt down before it. She then swept her clothing underneath her shins and sat on her insteps. Everything she carried, she slowly placed out in an orderly fashion by her side.

"Take off your messy swimsuit and put it that bin next to you," she said in a soft commanding tone.

*This isn't a swimsuit, woman. It's a battle suit.*

She smirked at me while I did my best to keep frustration from showing on my face.

I signed with exasperation. The suit was very difficult to take off—it clung to my body with suction as I slipped it down.

"Oh, let me help with that! There are microscopic plug-like projectiles attached to the inner membrane of the suit. They are plugged into your pores. A simple irritant mixed into your sweat should release them."

*I see. That explains why this suit feels like a second skin.*

The suit that was so well attached to me, it released with a lip-smacking sound, wherever it was pulled off. I peeled of the last of it, and my whole body felt relieved.

I have endured much hardship in my time, without much complaint. *Yet I must admit, that the odor of that animal was getting to me.*

*Sometimes I forget my womanly spirit, after so many eons of being constantly drenched with blood and flesh... of another.*

"Come." Tzwk smiled at me and motioned her hand. "Lay here." She pointed to the table.

*There is a sisterly air about her invitation. It is being projected from her soul in earnest. My instinct to quickly send someone into transition, at the smallest display of a threat, is diminishing.*

*This is not good—*

"*Stop* it!" She caught me in mid-thought with her words. "Sometimes it is good to feel like a vulnerable woman, even at the cost of your life."

*She is speaking to my essence, the pure innocent part of me cloaked in the garment of combat and bloodthirst.*

"Let me bathe you, and clear your consciousness." Her words removed a layer of resistance from my being. "I will not take away from your sword. I will sharpen it. It may make your stay easier."

The urge to speak left me and was replaced with the need to comply. I placed my hands on the edge of the table and sat down. She gently put her hand on my shoulder and pushed me down on my back.

*She is extremely strong. She could have forced me down easily…if she'd desired it.*

Her firm hand on my shoulder communicated so much. Trust being the main message.

"Can you remember the last time someone bathed you?" Tswk asked softly.

"No...yes." I am so disconnected from this world. My mother and my son's father. These are the only two in my whole span of years who come to mind.

"I will start with your head. Are you ready?" she spoke as if I was unaccustomed to bathing.

"Yes."

She reached over her side and picked up a blackcloth and folded it over. She then sprinkled gold and then indigo powder into it. Both had a strange luminesce to them.

Tzwk folded it once more then submerged it in the water. As she brought it up and wrung it out, small soap-like bubbles emerged from the cloth, giving off the scent of electricity and sesshni flowers merged together.

She proceeded to wash my face...and then something intriguing happened. My pores opened and began to secrete a sludge-like material.

I literally felt a breath of fresh air all about my body. I inquired about this, to my body, to innerstand the process taking place.

*Amazing.*

*The indigo colored particles in the soap act like magnets...drawing out the toxins and then feed off of them secreting a natural adhesive; along with more blackish sludge-like material.*

The gold particles followed by attaching themselves to the adhesive, and then funneled into my open pores, taking the shape of its walls—almost acting like insulated plating.

The sekhem of this planet was drawn towards me more than ever before. And the constant contemptous energy that has impinged against my body since I arrived here, melted away. Its attitude shifted from being defensive, to being tolerable of my prescence.

As it drew closer to my skin, it started to circle about: creating small vortexes of dynamic force.

"Take it in elder one." Tzkw commented softly and rested her hand on my shoulder.

The eyes of all these enumerable spirals pulled into my re-structured pores, and created vacuums—drawing in other surrounding energies in the room.

Throughout my body their presence traveled swiftly in my blood and fed receptors needed for my cells to communicate efficiently with this planet.

"The All Nature will not be as hostile regarding your existence," she said in a way as if she fully knew my plight.

*What is this sense of release I've experienced...the weight on my heart that has fueled my drive, my bloodthirst, has lifted....*

*What will I be without it?*

"Now I will cleanse your neck." said Tzwk knowingly.

The same process repeated itself as the firm strokes of the warm damp cloth brushed down the sides of my neck.

As I happened to glance over to the side, I noticed huge amounts of black sludge combined with soapy water make its way down canals leading to the furnace that heats the rocks.

Using the heightened perception of my body, I found that their function was more than just heating rocks. They were part of an intricate design that heats water into steam after it has been passed through a series of filters.

*I now see that the gratings below the rocks are piping allowing the refined water to pass through, and be released through miniature vents.*

*This purified steam passes through the heated rocks and combines with the steam created, when water was poured on them.*

*This room contains emotions and energies that have been transmutated into healing therapy in the form of mist. Allowing one to face themselves without any constraint of emotional blockage or defensive reactions.*

Everytime the soft and welcoming cloth glided down the side of my neck, I was reminded of all the desperate times when vicious hands were wrapped around them.

The times of combat that I'd waded through, had left hash memories...Memories that pressed into my skin and then into my soul.

I had not realized how they were shaping my path. Only the friction of my body striking against another was clear—all those times of being dragged by the scruff of my neck through battlefields littered with soldiers' corpses—some who sought fame by sticking their sword into bodies. Others who bared their bellies as the leaders of their families and culture.

In the end, they were all just empty shells.

When I reached their chiefs, it was not rare for me to be thrown to at their feet—to be done with as they pleased.

And just as often—much to these chiefs' surprise—to hear the sound of their throats opening... as they looked through a crimson cloud of blood at my detached expression.

My mind filled with past images collecting and purging through my skin, carrying with it the toxic energy of those times.

*What am I? Why do I love the feeling of an enemy under my heel?* Looking at Tzwk these questions seem to boil and rise to the surface of my lips.

"You are a warrior. You are an expression of expansion and contraction," she answered before I could ask. "Do not question yourself."

These words left her lips like rays from the sun.

Naturally. With clear purpose and intent.

"I will now cleanse your arms," Tzwk reached for my beckoning arm.

This time, the process began well before the cloth touched my skin. In fact, much more than a medium dispersion of sludge left it.

Huge globs of black grime forced their way out the pores of my arms, seeking to be free from confinement.

Even Tzwk, whom I surmise was well-versed in her craft, appeared surprised judging by the slight stiffening of her back. Although the look on her face remained the same, the minor tremor of her hand could be well read into.

Once she managed to gain her composure, she put the cloth down and grabbed generous portions of the gold and indigo powder in her hands. Without a second thought, she clutched my arm and began to remove the muck off me.

From shoulders to fingertips, she worked digligently to free my limbs from all the emotional toxins that gushed forth. Tzkw flung handful of clump after clump into the canals and as if alive, they responded by secreting water from their walls to dilute the sludge before it got to the filters.

A strong gust of steam shot forth from the heated boxes and filled the room with purified thoughts. I began to taste wet salt on my lips from tear ducts that had been dry for eons.

I watched Tzkw's movement as she practically scrapped the last bit of grime from my arms. *She is used to doing this for people, clearing away their weight. The motion of her arms and torque of her waist is elegant and light, attempting not to disturb the release of the one being bathed.*

*She has gained so much experience in her craft, it has become ingrained in her essence and being.*

"How have you lived so long and free at the same time carrying so much weight on your soul? Why have you allowed you body to become a dull and thick blunt blade?" she continued.

I listened as a babe would to its mother.

"You have neglected rest with The All Mind for an eternity just for the mere proof of your existence."

"Why?" she asked as if puzzled by my very existence.

*She sees through me with kindness and inner-standing. Yet I have the urge to rip her head off rather than appreciate it. She's like a worthy opponent exposing my weaknesses.*

"There is a serpent coiled around your heart. One that you feel you control."

The laughter that left her lips after that statement was so…so… *humbling.*

"You are not in control. You are addicted to its power. I cannot cleanse it from your heart. However I can make you its master. Come..." She motioned for me to rise and follow her.

When I stood up, light-headedness struck me along with the burning awareness of the presence of Apep more than ever before.

"Come Nth. The time is now." Tzkw said evenly, while I followed her lead.

She took my hand and lead me to the pool. Her physical contact grounded my steps and helped me to remain present.

I have not let anyone assist me in this manner since... *him.*

Khat had not indicated any sign of threats since we been here. In fact, this may be the first time in awhile that it has actually rested. While walking, I noticed that the canals, that were filled with sludge, were now without blemish or sign of moisture.

*I must admit that the construction of this house is dynamic and in synergy with the nature surrounding it. These beautiful wood floors are smoothed out with the same mixture that was used upstairs.*

Upon reaching the pool we both stood quietly next to one another and peered at his surface,

"Get in slowly. The water is hot...and alive" She said both welcomingly and with caution.

*Alive? Everything is alive.*

My bold step in, without testing her words for truth, was answered by Khat awakening and rapidly withdrawing my foot *fast.*

Strange, its reaction time was much slower than usual. *"This water's temperature is more than we are conditioned for to take all at once."* Khat was wide awake now. *"If you wish, I can shut down pain receptors, however we may damage our skin and will need additional time for new growth."*

I decided to be cautious about getting in on my second attempt. This time I placed my foot in toe first. The water began to move on its own to meet the rest of my foot. It literally swam up to my ankle.

I started to adjust to the high temperature...as the water gently drew my leg in. Little by little I was taken into the water by what appears to be a sentient consciousness.

"Sit," instructed Tzwk.

I knew she was aware that the water was already up to my chest, and that there was no seat in the pool.

*"Sit.* It will provide you a seat." This time she spoke more forcefully with her words.

As I lowered my body, the water level followed along. I felt support of some sort underneath my bottom. Although the flow was fluid, it still had a strong weighted presence around my body. I was being firmly embraced by the heat of the water on the surface of my skin.

"The rest of the cleansing must be done by you alone. Although you will face one of the fiercest battles in your life… you can handle it."

*I am almost afraid to respond.* "And what battle is that?"

"The battle to release all that pain that makes you who you

are." And with that, she sprinkled a generous amount of indigo and gold powders into the water.

The peacefully clear rippling waves gradually built to an incandescent green hue of strong ebbs and flows. Slowly from the other end of the pool, the height of the crests grew and bombarded my chest with stronger and stronger energies.

"Be strong…" Tzkw whispered on the air. She dimmed the light illuminated from the crystals, and left me in semi-darkness as she slipped out the room. As my eyes grew accustomed to the darkness two waves—about four feet in height— came crashing down on me.

There was nothing unsettling about this at all— even the fact that I was being pushed under by the repercussions of the impact, didn't not make me uneasy.

Gently yet with persistent force I was submerged deeper into the depth of the pool, which seemed to have gotten deeper than when I first set in it.

*Oddly enough, my body is not responding at all, in fact its complying. The will to fight back to the surface is being replaced by submission to the unknown.*

*I have never done this so consciously or willingly before...not since my first time coming into flesh.*

*Yet, I feel no apprehension about my limbs giving into the force imposed on them. Nor do I feel panicked about the fact that my body has not altered its respiratory function to breathe underwater.*

*I am...I am at peace.*

Looking at the painting on the ceiling through the glimmering surface of the water, reminded me of the many worlds I had sojourned on. Someone spent a great deal of focus and time filling in the canvas of the ceiling with realistic artwork of the night sky.

A beautiful pitch-black background and stars that appear like pinholes in darkness stretched across its face. Cosmic clouds of dust displayed ever so often across the landscape drew me into its imagery.

Lost in thought I didn't realize that the reason I didn't need to adjust to breathe underwater was because my lungs were filled with water.

Technically I'd drowned.

However, the water performed the function of my lungs by extracting the oxygen I needed from beyond its surface and feeding it into my bloodstream. Somehow my body cut my consciousness off, from realizing it and maintained limited functioning.

It had synchronized with the water and took in its consciousness…leaving me out.

Khat, on its own, succeeded in becoming one with the energy of its surroundings... where as before we were shunned from such a privilege.

I began to panic and called out desperately for Khat.

"*Khat! Khat! Ndjm E!*

*KhaT E Eu Nkht N Sekhmet N Ka.*

*Khat E Eu Jser N Ra N Ka.*

*Khat E Eu Nkht N Sekhmet N Ka.*

*Khat E Eu Jser N Ra N Ka.*"

Someone *else* was in the room!

"*Body!* Body! Hear me. My body is the might of Sekhmet's Spirit!" someone called out from outside the room mockingly. "My body is the Power of Ra's Spirit."

It was Jnfr translating my words.

"You can say it over and over again and none of it will work. Your words cannot reach where your body has risen" Jnfr went on and on like her mother.

*I am finding this family long-winded.*

"You might as well give up your personal war...with yourself."

Her words did not reflect the earlier demeanor of a child. And I heard all her words clearly from my watery bed.

*She must be using telepathy.*

Jnfr sat crouched over the pool with her hands on her knees, her figured rippled on the surface of the water. Swaying from side to side with a curious expression on her face, she peered into the water attempting to make out make my figure.

"Mother sent me down here to walk you through." Her voice seemed irritated. "Something about the projection of your energy down here made her think that without guidance you would threatened the structure of the house."

"Hilarious! What can you do? You were barely was able to handle Nnp and his kin."

I was just getting warmed-up. I would have had the whole lot begging for mercy in spite of my exhaustion.

"I thought I would humor mother by helping out. But now I am starting to see by the state of the water she may be right."

Jnfr was not using telepathy to communicate with me yet her words still reached me. "Nth, give up your personal war against yourself. If you can do that, then your body will fully embrace you again."

Every time she spoke, the water reacted to the tone of her voice by opening a small funnel between my ears and the surface allowing her voice to reach me.

*These beings have an uncanny natural synergy with their environment. Regardless of her heightened perception. I do not agree with her claim that I am at war with myself.*

*In fact, it is opposite of what she sees, I am in union with my body, we work as one and cannot be separated.*

"You are probably thinking that I am wrong," Jnfr said, reading my mind. "But I really do not have time or patience to convince you."

"Still I need to know what mother sees about you, in order for me to save you from leaving your body."

*What is it with the arrogance of this young woman— this child? I can never be separated from it.*

*Jnfr is naïve about a being like myself and my abilities. Khat and I have just been taken unawares since we have been on this planet...it happens. There is first time for everything.*

*I will have to force control and the only way to do that is to use the power of that venom that circulates in my bloodstream.*

*Focus. See the fire course through my arteries and veins. Call upon it to increase my body-heat and boil out this foreign water from my body.*

*The water that has embraced all the cells and channels in my body started to recede and leave. My organs once again returned their consciousness to me... to my mind...*

"DON'T GO ANY FURTHER!" yelled Jnfr. The vibrations from her yelling generated strong currents in the pool.

*What is...what is this? I was slipping losing the ties my thought had with Khat. What's happening?!*

I lost all connection to my body. I was fading. My body—Khat— did not respond to any of my calls. It is totally one with the water now.

And my summoning of Apep's venom did not change the situation at all. Regardless of it being helixed into every vessel, limb, extremity and organ of my body, especially in my heart.

My body and Apep's essence had taken leave of me, and express no need of my being to exist.

Just then Jnfr rose to her feet, hands outstretched. The water began to change its flow as several waterspouts swirled about and up out of the pool. They increased with speed spiraling upward towards Jnfr.

From I what I could make out, they attached themselves to her eyes, ears and center of her palms. As they attached to her, I felt a pinch inside my ears along with faint voice.

*She is using these spouts to communicate with me!* Her consciousness probed about in my mind, however I was unable to contact it directly.

"Mother is right. Women can ignore the sight of the heart. Nth, can you not see who this Pp, the serpent around your heart really is or are you just ignoring it?" She spoke directly to me—

to my heart.

"You cannot be whole until you accept yourself as a whole being. You have fought not to be separated from your body, so that your body can become a separate entity."

It was as if her words formed some type of medium between the cells of my body and my spiritual energy self. For the first time I saw through its eyes and recognized that my perception of our relationship was one sided.

*Khat, do you truly feel that way? That I have abused you and drove you to the stage you are in now...divorced from me?*

*That I have pulled away from my heart so that I would not endure its cycles. How can I communicate something to myself as if I were another entity? Why would I tell you these things when you are me?*

*Even this conversation is not truly taking place,*
*nor have the many before. Quite honestly, in my eyes I feel that I am unsettled and filled with doubt. That I must constantly ask myself what to do…and that I play a mental game of call and response in order to perform tasks that resulted from poor decisions…*

"*If I am not you then…Who are you?*" Khat replied.

With these deeply rooted words from Khat, I was the closest I ever been to being alone at the door to another life...what I heard some call on other worlds...

Death.

# N

No matter the situations endured in my time, I have withstood being pushed out my body and forced to rest in the bosom of Ntchr Neb. I always had an unrelenting will to live through my trials.

But now laying here submerged in water, the very thing that removed me from my body, no desire to continue came to my heart. I was humbled and beaten.

Living a falsehood for eternity only to satisfy my self-worth…to exist…now I was ready to leave.

"Stop being so melodramatic. You have just begun." Jfnr's words echoed through my head."You have the opportunity to start life anew…as a whole being."

"By admitting your humbled state, can't you sense how your body is returning to you?"

Jnfr's clarity of the situation renewed my spirit. Although her words were being communicated by the essence of the pool rather than actual words, I experienced their presence first in my ears and then in my heart.

And yes, I did see the webbing of my spiritual self being reached for by the Ra centers of my nervous systems.

They intertwined and meshed into the endings of one another like two hands folded together. My thoughts reverberated clearly, echoing their weight through my bloodstream and muscles.

I didn't sense the consciousness of Khat and myself separately…I only sensed…*myself.*

"Nth, you have taken the biggest step anyone can. The realization of self. Now you must forgive your son's father."

These words…those simple words from this child's mouth shook me harder than anything ever spoken to me. Had I gone mad? Or had I purposefully disillusioned myself?

*Sa Sekhmet's father was Apep. Apep is…is my husband. Or should I say my husband brought Apep into physical being through his actions.*

One moment that lacked discernment on his part caused a snowball effect of tragic and undesirable outcomes. My husband's bite was one out of love and desperation—the liquid in his venom, the tears his soul could no longer cry.

*And, now I cry them for him.*

"Nth, are you ready to become whole once more?" She asked in earnesty.

"Yes, I am ready. Dear child, I AM READY," the ability for speech had returned to me.

"Now the serpent will be yours." The strength carried in her words hung in my thoughts.

Jnfr released the connection between us and the spiral-like vessels whipped back into the pool.

The venom, which always shone a dangerous red each time I was approached the beserker state, now radiated a strong indigo hue free of chaos.

I was now closer to the essence of it than ever before. For an instant I saw my body—my spiritual body— and Apep in an embrace that defies words.

My spiritual body appeared as an orange lioness forming the outer skin of my entire being, with a golden Apep wrapped around her limbs, embracing them like muscle tissue becoming like a living armor.

*Yet, I now see this is not Apep anymore.*

*This is Wadjet, who has evolved out of the result of Apep finding peace with all things.*

Once the vision faded, I remained as Neith, not Neith and her inconquerable Khat. Just Neith.

The water that brought me through my passage of growth, exited out my pores joining the rest of the body of water in the pool. It solidified underneath me and pushed me up to the surface like a rising platform.

As my face pushed through the membrane of water, I gasped like I took my first breath of air.

"Well get up and come over here," said Jnfr, motioning for me to come over to her.

I rose up somewhat sluggishly getting used to my body's refreshed structure. My limbs moved with a higher sense of freedom; and the heightened awareness of things around me was intoxicating. Jnfr held her arms out to embrace me— arms that I could not wait to hold me.

"I am taking her now! We waited long enough! Fight all you *want!*" a voice yelled out from behind the entrance's flaps.

Just when I had a moment of clarity, chaos followed not too far behind.

*Well, that's nothing new, nothing new at all.*

Two bodies burst through the flaps embraced in struggle: one Tzwk and the other a huge male.

What a stench.

Their tangled bodies rolled about on the sauna room's floor. The floor board creaked from the weight of their struggle. It was evident that this huge man's size, matched his physical strength. Once he was able to get his body into the fight, Tzkw would be at a disadvantage.

All I could do was watch while I readjusted myself to my cleansed body.

## *Chapter Medju*
## *Purpose*

*I can't just sit here and punch on this woman's kidneys all day. Especially when she re-directs the force of the blows back at me.*

*The one I want is just a few feet away from us.*

*But she might as well be a mile away with the struggle this woman is putting up.*

*Crap.*

The heat of The Fever was rising— I was becoming filled with the urge to take life. *Please not now!*

Although I had her arms pinned underneath my knees, she was slowly inching up to position herself to put me at a disadvantage. Yet, I had an advantage. The Fever.

*I'll knock her out using the increased strength that it feeds me with each passing moment.*

*Damn—waited too long!*

Somehow she'd figured out my intentions and slid her

arms free from my knees.

*She's quick. All I saw was a flash of something. Could have been her arms.*

Ringing. A strong ringing suddenly filled my ears.

She moved so quick! That when she clapped my ears. I'd reacted a second too late to block them.

*She ruptured my eardrums—I know she did!*

My breathing grew shallow and I wanted to vomit. My ears dripped blood, pieces of my eardrum tissue oozed out while I was getting myself together to subdue her.

The pain was so intense that my temperature skyrocketed—triggering the rapid regeneration of lost tissue in the process. She tried to get completely from under me while I was disorientated by the pain, a pain that seemed almost orgasmic.

I found myself wanting her to share in it. This feeling reminded me of fights with my wife—fights that once were part of our foreplay. Straddled over her body on the floor, just as I was now. And like then, my thoughts wander because I am in control.

*She's going nowhere, no matter how much she struggles.*

Dominance over another became a habit of mine. A habit that went too far and eventually brought about The Fever. I remember wrapping my arms around her neck and watching her gasped for air...

*Damn! This woman's been beating my forearms something fierce and coughing.*

I was choking her the whole time. I didn't realize it, until I looked down and saw my hands around her neck.

Her face was bruised, it wasn't before. I must have blacked out and struck her; then dragged her back underneath me. I didn't want this. I didn't want to re-live those wicked actions anymore.

I should have refused Drn's offer. At least I would have been with the All Nature instead of fighting off the inevitable.

"You will not succeed in my husband's *will...!*" Her gurgling voice carried a tone of resolve.

The tissues in my ears must have just finish regenerating for me to make out the dull sound of her voice.

"I will let you experience the pain of my heart's scar before this night is out!" she cried.

All around us the air began to draw in and compress against our bodies.

She was gathering in the forces around us. She took a deep breath, and then clutched my hands with massive strength. When she yanked my arms from her neck, my joints almost gave way! She used them as a support to pull herself out from between my legs.

*Ugggbhhh!*

*My arms...my arm muscles and nerves have been crushed against my bones.*

I trembled from the wrist down, trying to work my hands to grab her. My fingers were next to useless.

And my situation was about to get worst. Her daughter and a petite little girl, who were just looking on at first, seemed to have decided to head over to us.

*I need to finish her now.*

The elbow to her face only added to her ability to channel kinetic force, which she used it to strike my back. She got around behind me. After that, she rammed another knee into my lower back forcing me to fall forward and smash my face. I fought to stay conscious... until her strikes to my pressure points and joints convinced me sleep was better.

It was only The Fever that kept me aware, with a fighting spirit. Immediately, she wrapped her arm around my throat and pushed my neck into the crease of her arm by nudging the back of my skull with her chin.

She squeezed with her all her might—pushing forward from her hips.

*Strangulation.*

My arms flayed about on their own. Then my body's natural survival instinct moved past my conscious thought, and forced the density of my muscles to cover over my vessels and nerves, so that I still might have some amount of air traveling to my head.

"He's tensing! Give me the spike plant powder! *Now!*" Her words literally shot across the room to her daughter.

*She's quick.*

With a blinding speed, she released her hold and swung her fist into the back of my head. She must have struck my brain stem because I couldn't move to respond.

Her daughter, whizzed passed us, ran into a hidden room and came back out with a pouch. She joined her mother, who still remained straddled over me, and rubbed silvery powder, from the pouch, on her mother's arm.

Just as I recovered from being disorientated, she resumed her stranglehold with added vigor.

*I must force her into a stalemate, and when has she loses her stamina, I'll simply flip her over and knock her out. The others I can deal with easily—only two girls.*

Although it was challenging to focus having my air supply cut from me, I still managed a few bursts of The Fever to deal with the strangulation.

Every time I fought, I was always surprised by the speed of my thoughts and my movements. *Come on Dvln, stay focused! Quit with your introspective thoughts. You are fighting, not sidelining!*

"The Fever is no direct fault of your own. It is something between you and your mate that is unresolved." Her words interupted my thoughts. "Your only blame is not doing anything to fix it"

There were many things that she could have whispered into my ear at this moment— 'You are going to die' or 'I will send you to the unknown'— to me would have been more appropriate; especially given the seriousness of the matter.

But to say something that dealt with my personal issues, was so...compassionate. Nevertheless, I was still going to carry through with my mission.

"For your sake. I will release you."

I didn't know exactly what that meant, but I it was too close to, 'You are going to die,' for my comfort. I needed to burst no–

*Arrgggh!*

Something stabbed me all around in my neck, piercing into the extra skin and muscle walls I generated. I was not being strangled. She was trying to take my head off!

## N

*I have to relax and regain my focus.*

*Nnnnnn—too much, too much pressure!*

"Ngln, I am sorry!I'm...!" with what little breath I had, I screamed out with what might be my final words.

Thoughts of my wife flooded my mind. *I will never be able to redeem myself.*

"Jnfr, Nth, get into the water. Do it *now!* Stay clear of us!" she screamed out to the girls.

"But...!" The one I was here for stood frozen, trying to utter words from her mouth.

The other grabbed her and pulled them both in the pool. There must be something this woman sensed about me that made her warn the others the way she did.

Whatever that may be mean nothing to me. I will burst, knock out this woman and subdue the child. My mission will be complete and I will be able to spend my final days with my son; fulfilled in my duty.

The Fever is rising. The inside of my bones feel like liquid magma flowing through them. My blood boiled with the fiery untamed side of the All Nature.

"So, you have made your decision—as I have made *mine!*" the woman screamed.

*Nnnnnnn!* Once again, something was pushing out the

pores of her arms deeper into my neck.

*I must do it now, before I'm beheaded. I must f*ully burst.

"Listen up...and try not to panic. I am going to severe your head, before it explodes and takes this whole house with it," she spoke without emotion, as if it was a part of her daily duties.

This whole time I was pretty much resolved myself, Yet this woman's demeanor was *unnerving*. What she just spoke of, strangely brought to mind, a memory.

An element like a fuse connected to another element that would explode with a huge impact. Yet, I have never experienced anything like that on this world—something that would bring about that much destruction, intentionally.

"Your body," she continued with more of her verbal torture, "will be incernerated along with mine. The Fever will make sure of that."

She paused then continued. "But, since your head will be separated from your body, you will have a few moments of clarity in this physical world."

Suddenly, I became numb to the physical world and more aware of the pain in my heart and mind.

Out her mouth came more unwavering words: "I suggest that you make peace with anything that had brought you to this state, before the next world greets you," she finished, closing herself off to continue with her work.

When her lips met and sealed her mouth, my feet burst into flame and quickly ate through my flesh to the bone. My clothes caught fire, despite their flame-resistant fibers.

I inched my neck to turn as much as I could, moving almost one by one against the numerous miniature dagger-like projectiles driving into my neck. Severing all tissue, flesh, muscle and other parts that kept my head attached. Once my feet were gone, it left an impression of ash and flesh burnt into the floor.

My inflamed clothes crept up the rest of my body, igniting everything in its path. The woman's simple one-piece housedress—although possessing the same flame resistant material as mine—caught fire as well. She did not pay it any attention.

She simply worked quicker to force my head off, while my body worked twice as hard to keep it attached. At this point, any voluntary control of my cellular density was claimed by the survival instinct of my body. It sought to keep me alive until my head was detonated.

My heart raced, pumping the fear of the inevitable throughout the remainder of my body. I wanted to turn my head away from the sight, but couldn't. It would be locked into place for the rest of this nightmare.

## N

*I am just too calm. Just too accepting of things, that I know I can change. That's my life.*

I reluctantly watched my legs eaten away by the flame, my blood spilling out for but a moment before it became ash. My organs spilled out for but a second before they too became ash.

Her body burnt slower than mine, although it still succumbed to the flame. She was close to my cervical bone, *I can feel my sinews and flesh tearing away from the rest of my neck.*

Her vigilance overcame all attempts of my body, and pierced through all obstructions. *But I am not scared anymore. Her desperation in violently tearing my head off was...compassionate. Like she is granting me an honorable death and an opportunity for redemption.*

I felt no heat...no heat..only a slight warmth as I rolled away from her and my body.

The sound of bone being sawed through rattled me but for an instant. Then was replaced by the freedom from The Fever.

She let go and crawled away slowly from my flaming carcass, leaving a trail of her own smoldering flesh in the process.

*My body makes one final burst of flame that engulfs the whole room, laying everything down its path with searing heat and concussive force...*

The ones in the pool ducked into it just in time to avoid

the onslaught that nearly destroyed everything else in this room. It also blasted a hole clear through the ceiling before dying out and leaving a pile of ash and embers.

She looked at the pile of my remains then at me.

"Do you see them? Look quickly before they are gone!"

I look again and saw what looks partially familiar and foreign at the same time. Red bodies of light and mist whirling about my remains. Their frames expanded and contracted hovering over whatever embers that still glowed.

*Breathing. They're breathing in The Fever.*

Once all light was gone—or should I say eaten— the room grew near pitch black. The Tkkn in the corners, completely depleted of energy, left the room looking more like a tomb.

The red spirit-like things having no need to be present left through the hole in the ceiling.

*I would swear one looked back at me...*

Maybe it was the lack oxygen and blood. I felt at peace, but fading from this world.

"The Fever is gone. Has not some of your humanity returned? Your willful spirit? Enough to call me by my name?" she spoke softly to me with a light gurgling in her throat.

Her will was indomitable, she sat cross-legged covered in flame, her flesh gradually being eaten away to the bone.

Somehow she is able to diminish the rate that her flesh was consumed, along with managing to console...me.

My voice was even raspier than hers. "Tzkw...how are you able to do these things?"

"Unimportant. No time for that. Stretch your spirit to my hand."

Without hesitation, I extended my spirit toward her as she asked. All that made me who I am, gathered about my severed head and shot out towards her.

*I see myself leaving my last body part through new eyes as I made my way to Tzkw.*

The life that filled my physical eyes was pulled along with me. I landed in her hand, having an entirely new form.

*I cannot see it myself. I can only expect that it must be pure, since she looked down at me like I was a newborn.*

*I feel safe.*

She smiled.

"I did my best to protect my family on what I now remember to be our home world," I said. "And when we perished...I now see it was just our time to go."

I communicated the rest to her without moving my lips ...watching her spirit glow stronger as her body disintergrated. *I provided financial security, shelter, food and clothing—lavishly. Yet, I did not give my heart. I want to give it now.*

These things I did not know before. And now, I know them intimately while I pulsed in Tzkw's palm.

She looked up into the opening of the ceiling, raising her left arm. An indigo stream of light beamed through and current of energy swirled about it.

Her focus was the interrupted. She turned to the pool. "Stay back the both of you. Do not come here no matter what your see or feel."

Her jaw fell and evaporated in midair before it could hit the floor. For Tzkw and myself, these things brought us little pain because we were now operating from another scale of life.

*Nevertheless, this must be hard on her daughter.* She screamed out and tried to rush from out the pool. Her wet body caused her to slip back in—giving the little girl with her enough time to keep her still.

Satisfied, Tzkw turned her attention back to me. "Can you see her. See your wife, Ngln?"

I looked up into the spinning sphere that formed in the opening of the ceiling and saw a sight that would have caused tears... if I had them.

I saw Ngln. My wife.

It was not her physical body that I perceived. Nor was it a

light form of a body. Something welled up in my being causing me to feel a familiarity of energy.

It was *her.*

"Go to her and regain your balance."

And with that I was pulled through Tzkw's right palm, witnessing spiritual matter and flesh disattaching themselves from one another, as I traveled through her, and then spiraled up her left arm and palm towards the light.

To Ngln.

*I lookj at Tzkw, to see her smile up at me...her body engulfed by flames...*

## *Chapter Medju Wa*
## *Apep*

*She is near. I can feel her.*

*And she is—different. I do not run alongside her as I did before.*

*What has become of her?*

*No matter, we shall meet again and I will have her this time for eternity. Meanwhile, I will gather followers to this small burnt rock.*

It had been a day since I lay coiled up in one position here on the ground, not moving, the smells of singed rock, trees and foliage my only company.

And I hungered.

I desired flesh that was tempered by the challenges of the environment that gave birth to it. A creature that had some measure of dominion over this area and others.

Anything short of this, would only prolong my hunger.

# N

After my long journey of pursuit through the dark skies of space, I was drained of vitality and drive. Every part of my being sort to recover and grow new flesh. Nothing more.

Hunting was unthinkable.

So I lay in a coil, parts of my skin scorched, exposed to attacks from all manner of beasts, large and small.

And they came...raking their claws against my flesh, driving their fangs into my sides and snapping their pinchers into my scales.

I endured their onslaught, waiting for one that was worthy of my fangs.

Then suddenly they yielded in their attacks—seeing that there was no way for them to make me submit—and their own fear was driving them mad, the scent of it poured heavy from their pores.

I did not have to wait long, because he came and we fought. Tooth and claw. At the end he—their mightiest— was crushed...freed of all breath and swallowed whole.

It was then, that all who bared their teeth, sheathed them and recognized me as their better...their ruler.

It was also at this time, that I recognized the consciousness of this rock and its disdain for its invaders. I, being one of them. It had the power yet no authority to strike me.

I had no bond to any immediate authority yet my power paled by comparison.

A stalemate. The one I'd swallowed was called *Nnp*, a large tasty dog. Now, I lay here alert and poised.

His kinsman kneeled before me. Some cautiously approached with their heads bowed.

They began to lick clean my wounds, inflicted by Nnp, their former ruler. I allowed them to do this, thinking that it might make my dominion over them easier.

Yet, I did not dropped my awareness for one instant. *They may still try to bite into my flesh.*

They stopped in unison and raised their heads. Given their grim expressions and shift in scents, I could tell they'd gained some knowledge about me from the taste of my blood.

In an instant, they withdrew their spirits to a place I could not follow.

Even though I now commanded them, I still did not have complete rulership over them.

Rulership was what I wanted.

*Wait. One of their younglings is missing. I do not sense his scent nearby.*

Once the others realized that I knew one of their brethren was gone, they quickly vanished along with him.

*Strange.*

*They have not moved from this place...even though I can not sense them at all. They are still here, my intuition tells me so.*

The winds moved about freely about, unfettered by anything except by my body and the smoldering stumps around me. Regardless of this, I know they were still there... in front of me circling about, quietly looking for some weakness in my guard.

*This rock itself is foreign to me, but there is an essence or essences on it that are familiar to me. Very close in relation to the ones from the place I called home.*

*The blue rock.*

The soil underneath me here on this rock, might as well be empty space, for it provided no welcome to my body. Nothing but a surface, which my body opposed weight on it, rather than being by supported it.

I am unable to talk to the nature around me and it purposely sealed its words from me.

But, as I took in the flesh and spirit of Nnp, I slowly gained some small link with this environment.

"Why did you your change your appearance?" I said. "Do you think I am unaware that you are still there?" I took care to speak confidently.

"I can *see* you.You, the big one, come here."

I called out to the air, as if I spoke directly to him—suggesting I could see their difference in size.

One of them relaxed their stance enough to breathe. Not just in the normal sense. No, he released his breathe into this realm from the one he'd *retreated* to. Then retreated to it once more.

The rest of his pack continued in that place I couldn't follow into.

But his momentary release was enough for me to locate him, and whip my tail around his hulking mass.

I swiftly constricted my body after I coiled in on him, hugged him until I felt muscle pressed against bone. Giving him no time to struggle.

"Tell me where the small one went!" I commanded.

"Master," he spoke through gasps of breath, "although you command our spirits for battle having usurped our ruler, Nnp, you have no command over our hearts!"

*"Ha Ha Ha!"* my laughing constricted my body tighter around him with each bellow. "You have mistaken my intentionssssshh...What I have asked and will ask is all preparation for battle!"

"To send you into battle against my enemy—the

one you attempt to hide from me. I can see in Nnp's memory a glimpse of the one I seek. Yet it is clouded, being purposely hidden every time I seek to read it."

For a moment, the others became visible to my senses, then faded away once more. The collective tension released in their scents moved swiftly through the air, and allowed me to track their location with ease. I must have struck a nerve for them all to be so careless as a group.

"I see." I let the dog go—but not before crushing his body within an inch of his life.

I flung him to where I now knew the majority of his pack stood. He smashed into two or three with so much force, that it caused them to lose focus and appear visible.

*Apparently the place they retreated to does not fully envelop their bodies.*

Gradually more and more of them came from out the folds... first as a small sphere of dust, then as a black blob of spirit force...then lastly into their full bodies.

*I see them. Their numbers have grown, much more than they first started with! They have been calling for reinforcements this whole time!*

One approached me. Judging by his demeanor and scent, he seemed to be Nnp's successor. His mass was almost as large as his former leader's, yet his spirit carried less charisma. He posed no threat to me and he knew it.

"Please stop this!" he pleaded. "If you persist you will cause much chaos, then be dealt with by the All Nature! Chaos that will have a heavy toll on our land!"

This idealist seemed to have much to say. His babble became tiresome quickly. "The All Nature?" I questioned.

*The children here only know their parent, as much as the parent allows them to know. But, I know their parent from the perspective of being a parent myself.*

"Yes, the presence and sum totality of all things on this world." he continued yammering. "The one that even you must fear."

*Fear?*

I bit deep into his hind quarters. He struggled to free himself, but only added to the look of anguish on his face. I drove the fang that snared him deeper into his flesh, and swung my head so his body pivoted: bringing us eye to eye.

The girth of my fang along with its grinding against nerve and muscle, forced him to be docile. I wanted him to know that although I have no power over this All Nature, I certainly had dominance over the lives of his pack.

"No more talk of this All Nature!" I commanded with their second dangling from my mouth.

They all drew back from me, scraping and dragging the scorched earth with their paws.

"Now, go find the one I am looking for and bring her to me... reasonably alive!"

When I shook the dog off my fang, he slid down off it and plopped down in front of me.

"And take this proud one with you!"

All the while as I spoke, I noticed they all faded in and out testing my claim—the claim that I could see them.

They dragged their wounded by the scruff of his neck along the ground as they departed. His limp body pulled along the black soil, creating a trail that lead back into my territory.

*I will have to change that.*

I waited a few moments then followed. As I moved, the pain of my wounds finally began to seep in. Once I seen the trail thin out and meld into the plush grass floor that filled this area, I turned back facing the direction from which I came.

I quickly side-winded back to my domain, using my body to brush away the trail left by the dogs. When I arrived back, my body throbbed and stung all about.

I almost drifted to sleep; which is the natural reaction of my body when I am wounded to this extent. I only remained awake due to the nourishment I was receiving from Nnp.

Without further hesitation, I reared my head up allowing the rest of my body to follow the rising of it. Once I gained enough height, I drove my head into the soft earth. My initial drive took me a few feet into the ground.

I continued this until I penetrated deep enough to contact soft earth. Moving through, I cleared away rock and sediment, all the while fighting my urge to slumber.

I fashioned a few chambers, hollowing out the earth with my mass and firmly packing the loose dirt with my tail end, against what would become walls.

*This underground lair will serve as my base of operations during my capture of that wild one...my wife.*

When the word *wife* formed in my thoughts, I was quickly taken back to a time long ago, when I possessed a body and limbs of a man...

I remembered holding her, and rubbing her belly that held our son inside.

*She is the one who spat me out as I am today. And today…I have no attachment to it—that time. It is dark and cold to me like my surroundings.*

*Yes. The dampness brings me back to who I am presently...one who challenges balance and turns all on their ear who think they are virtuous.*

*I will strike at this world as I have done on the past one. Yet, the time comes soon for me to shed this skin. Until that moment I will rest...*

## *Chapter Medju Senu*
## *Another*

This other addition appeared to be more bothersome than the first. It seemed to be the complement of the one called *Neith.*

I had an urge to crush this serpent yet, it was more in tune with my body than the latter.

Apep, the name whispered by its heart, was more suited for my coming task than anyone else on my body. Not quite an animal, but not quite what you could call human.

Then again, the ones you think are human are much more than that, as you and Neith will soon discover.

Apep innerstands his body and purpose intimately, although it was a path chosen out of desperation. Even though I did not find him the most hospitable being, he may sit in my flesh without any intervention from me.

I will ignore his boasts and taunts. I am interested in seeing if he may be suitable for my needs in the future.

Surprisingly, Neith does not bare the same amount of repelling energy from before. She is almost... *tolerable*. Her experience with that mother and daughter has brought her to realizations that a being like herself should have long resolved.

Such arrogance! To think she tortured herself for eons into thinking she was advanced, by driving her physical shell into a separate conscious!

Had I done the same— during my time as a being like Neith— I would have never risen up the rungs of life as I have.

She is not the same eyesore that I wanted to scratch off my surface. Yet, those illusions she created did give her an edge. Does she still possess the same fortitude, as she did in her previous incarnation?

I wonder.

Would she be suitable for the task at hand?

Maybe.

Time after time I looked across my lands—my skin— and saw all that has been good these many cycles. Even after the coming of my sister's children.

My body has remained in balance, in this house of the *Fiery Ones*. I have received their warmth and produced life. My waters cooled as my face turned away from them, and heated when I faced him.

The love that they shared, has caused many forms to spring forth from my surface over the ages. The wet ones, gills and fins. The high ones, wings and beaks. The ones of the ground, claws and teeth. Existing and striving for an endless variety of cycles, coming and going, taking and receiving.

Yes! I have enjoyed much during my spinning and my time for judgment approaches.

My test.

Will I continue in this vessel or move on? I've had my fill of joy in this form and I have no regrets. Although each time I was born into another form, my past was erased.

I worked countless eons to recall those experiences. I remembered when I was but an insect—when I crawled about in an infinite world of predators, including nourishing entities.

So I know well the challenges and joys of those that crawl upon my surface. The same can be said for the many other creatures that inhabit my body.

Through my many life cycles and experiences, I was being reared to become a parent and sustainer of many lives.

When my sister's children, your brothers and sisters, came to me, I endowed them all with a bountiful amount of spark—

what you may call carbon or melanin to deal with the harsh environment of my body. And to know and communicate with all essences around them. Some were naturally able to conduct this gift, while others were unable to let go of their past regrets. Regrets that blocked them from growth.

Those beings eventually regressed into a more primal attitude, which developed in what they called *The Fever.*

And there were others who never entered into my atmosphere as physical beings—those ones who fed off the energies of The Fever, and the blaze created by their bodies in flames.

Much of this avoidable through slow removal of the chemical programming and memory patterns, in their biological makeup over generations.

Are you following along? Or do you still think you are just reading a science fiction novel—critiquing everything being said, based on your worldly knowledge?

I shall continue.

Each being on this planet has led many lifetimes, enough for the process of removal to take effect.

But, I chose not to meddle directly with the only thing that made your kind what it was.

*Will.*

# N

No other beings have entered my body since their arrival, so the processes of life continued with a definite outcome.

That was until the arrival of Apep and Neith.

I know, that as you are reading these pages, you cannot comprehend the time that has passed within a blink of an eye. But, that is absolutely what took place, an eye blinked behind what you call the sun.

And when it opened my sister's children were with me.

In my house, time is incalculable by any of your engineered standards of measurements. At best, your scientists are still guessing and becoming more psychic in their pursuit to make their visions realities.

I will allow you to dwell on that for a moment.

It must also be said that once your kind came to me, they were flushed clean of mental parasites such as racism and sexism. Much of these inbred corruptions were purged from their blood.

But your regrets were another matter.

N

## *Chapter Medju Shemet*
## *Eye*

The light of the dawn poured through the gaping hole in the ceiling, dust that settled seemed to spring up with life floating about in the light.

Jnfr and I looked at one another, we knew it was safe to come out of the pool. But we both seemed to be weighted down.

As we climbed out, the water quickly dripped off both of our bodies—more so off Jnfr because she was still wearing clothes. The room was slightly chilly which added to the overall mood.

We both stop moving when our eyes fixed on the same sight. Tzkw.

Tzkw continued to burn away slowly, as the flame's heat

became less intense with each passing moment. A sad feeling came over me and my face became warm with tears long forgotten.

These kind of tears I'd wept for one other that possessed this level of compassion. My own Mut, my mother.

I held Jnfr close to me, embracing her as much as my smaller frame could handle. I gently sat us down on the floor; where there wasn't broken wood and scattered furnishings.

Jnfr clutched nervously at my arm, I rocked us both back and forth as we watched the blaze become dimmer and dimmer. She convulsed and coughed the way any child would at such a sight.

She picked up that I was watching her intently, and started to bite her lower lip to hold herself back from bursting into tears. When she began to bleed from unconsciously biting so hard, I squeezed the sides of her jaw tightly to get her to release her lip.

Her lip plopped out of mouth—punctured in the middle by her teeth. She gasped deeply, then dropped her head, letting go of all the tension in her upper-body. I looked down at her in my arms, and saw that she'd come to a restful position.

I glanced at Tzkw. Her body was almost gone.

She sat upright with her legs crossed, the incandescent hue

of her body traveling between spectrums.

"I do not have much time." Her mental projections had the same effect as her physical voice. "I want to give you each, one of my eyes"

She lifted up her arm, and what little bit of flesh and bone remained quickly melted away into liquid... then ash. All that was left was an astral equlivalent of a limb. In fact, what was left of her body was a mixture of melted flesh and bone with astral limbs protruding from them.

She motioned with her spirit-like fingers for us to come over to her. When I finally got Jnfr to her feet, her body slumped over my side.

She offered no assistance, only dead weight. We shuffled over to her mother, every few steps Jnfr almost collapsed from heartache. It was only the voice of her mother that carried her the distance.

Walking over to Tzwk became a workout, since I was not fully recovered from my transition. I dragged her limp eight foot body across the floor, that was littered with debris and shards of wood sticking out of it.

*I'd rather face five hungry dogs from Nnp's pack even with my strength depleted.*

"Sit..." Tzkw instructed.

She lowered her arm in front of her, the motion resulted in the rest her body finally disintegrating into ash. Jnfr fell to her knees and scraped at the floor with her nails.

She went to wrap her arms around her mother only to end up embracing herself. The rapid motion of her arms passing through air, scattered what little bit of ashes piled in front of her.

Tzkw's body gradually reincorporated after being dispersed by Jnfr's failed hug attempt.

*I am at a loss of words. It never seems to surprise me how much people with evolved spirits and minds, have the hardest time communicating their feelings.*

*Seeing mother and daughter operate perceptions that misinnerstand each other proves that point.*

"Child, do not carry on so... I am you and always will be with you." But Tzkw's lofty words did not give the child any consolation.

She needed to lament, to grieve, rather than to grasp the severity of her situation. A heavy rush of tears followed covering Jnfr's face—dropping like rain whenever she shook.

I reached out for her shoulders and pulled her into my lap. She rubbed her cheek against my thigh sniffling, trying to hold her emotions in. I stroked her thick hair, and rubbed the curls against her scalp, the way my mother once did for me as a child.

"Jnfr, Jnfr..." I whispered her name in her ear, over and over, to bring her back into the present.

She shook her head in "No," gestures in my lap then screamed and kicked her legs.

Murmuring in a low voice followed her head shakes: "Noooooo...*Nooooooo!*" then jammed her elbows into my naked body, leaving dark marks across my brown skin.

*"Jnfr!"* I raised my voice which jarred her out of her tantrum and helped to preserve my beautiful skin. "Your mother is there in front of us—*look!*"

Her time for lament was over. Jnfr raised her head slowly, her chin trembled as she fought to keep it still.

I noticed my usual scorn for being thrusted into situation after situation without rest, did not surface. In fact, it was nonexistent.

Suddenly, my hairs stood on end, warmth spread across my scalp, my ears, brow and nose, then finally my entire face.

Tzkw was now behind us, embracing us both with her astral like arms. It was more evident now than before that Tzkw was a master of spiritual arts— she must be.

The ability to affect the physical realm or even become solid, involves the knowledge of natural forces coupled with a strong will. Throughout this whole ordeal she remained unconditionally resolved and unnerved.

*Yet something— one thing— still keeps her anchored in this realm.*

"The scar on my heart, still weighs heavy," she spoke softly as if in response to my thoughts. She pulled us tighter together, her words taking on a stronger resonance in my skull. I felt the pulsing of energy from her astral body against my skin.

It was like feeling blood course through the body when you held someone close.

"However, I am ready to let go. Once I do that, I will not be bound to this fold of our world any longer." The tone of her voice swayed between emotions.

Jnfr continued to sob and shake, not finding much comfort in her projected words.

Tzkw exhaled in disappointment.

I remained silent, unable to say anything to match her yammering—knowing too, that my thoughts were heard loudly.

And then...

"Give us your eyes and be done with all this." These words left my mouth effortless, along with the stern energy that carried them. "No one appreciates your long drawn out exit…except you." I finished.

Although my words were harsh, they were spoken with

earnest compassion.

*I have been at the crossroads were Tzkw now stands, and need not be reminded of them.*

*There is pain.*

*Pain that is only generated by holding on to something we cannot change.*

*I remember well, my numerous escapes from Ammitt's jaws, before reconstituting my body.*

*And sitting here now, allowing her to go and go is disrespectful of everything that she has done for me. It is disrespectful to the cleansing of my soul, and the time she took to literally scrape away at the grime on both my body and spirit.*

*She has etched an immeasurable gratitiude on my heart.*

"You innerstand my words Tzkw, yes? I will watch over your daughter and end your husband's pain."

"Indeed...sister." Tzkw's astral form faded away as the words left her lips.

Suddenly I felt something push gently against my skin—something not quite corporeal. It continued to push further, and entered every layer of my skin...bit by bit.

My naked body was being affected allover. A chill ran through it, much more than the chill I experienced after leaving the pool and not drying off. The gentle pushing became more insistent, rushing through all the parts of my being...in and out of every cell...traversed between the small spaces that held them together.

It was Tzkw. Her essence— her being—left a trace of itself in every part of our structures.

I am sure the same thing was happening to her, because she calmed down dramatically. It was as if all the anchors in every small part of my being were lifted...and then suddenly dropped.

Tzkw appeared in front of us once again. She faced us and placed her hands to our face. And it was over.

Yet I had the feeling something was added to right side of my head and at the same time something removed.

*She left something in us, something we will need, very soon.*

I looked about and out my left eye saw things I could not readily put into words. I saw beyond the destruction that filled the room.

From out of the rubble, astral-like images emerged, images of Tzkw and Jnfr working on their hands and knees. Both of them hard at work smoothing out the floors, taking great pride in their task.

Jnfr was smaller than she is now and had a more youthful look on her face. Tzkw's facial expression was free-spirited and did not carry the burden I saw when I first met her.

These images appeared to be attached to the floor by some type of psychic webbing that swayed and pulsed along with their motion.

*The more I observe it the more becomes apparent that these are memories...memories of the room.*

Suddenly, the light radiating around these memories turned murky brown and then bright red as an ominous figure entered the scene. And then the images abruptly evaporated.

I experienced some sense of withdrawal when the memories ceased to play. And a need to see more, to be sure that it did not escalate to where I thought it was heading.

Entranced and almost chemically dependant on what I witnessed, I didn't notice that Tzkw was no longer amongst us. The warm physical impressions that her presence gave off left our surroundings, although her essence was now imbued into both our bodies.

The room seemed darker and lifeless, the damaged furnishings gave off a cold aura. The vibration given off by the broken floors boards and scattered rubble laid about, increased the overall build up of depressed psychic energy.

*Since I have been on this world, I have noticed the*

*powerful psychic energy coupled with the raw sekhem that fills the atmosphere.*

*But, due to my recent transitions and with the added eye from Tzkw, I am becoming more and more impaired by their waves. Maybe that's the reason behind the emotional withdrawal I experienced earlier.*

*In any case, I just located the plane to place my bodily and spiritual functions to rest at, to avoid interference.*

The tussle between Tzkw and the smelly male had literally tore the room apart. They'd smashed the bench that helped rebirth me. In addition to their combined weight and force ripped up the floor.

We'd stood in the pool witnessing all that took place, without lending any aid. Not that it would have been accepted. Tzkw had possessed more than the necessary skills to defeat her attacker.

But she'd decided to also cure him and end the current cycle of *her* life too. It was as if she knew that these moments would lead into her new life.

*Is that what it means to be truly immortal? A true being of cosmic awareness? Ntchru?*

While I was lost in contemplation, Jnfr slipped away back to the pool. I got up and walked over to her. After the first few steps, I saw my battle suit sprawled out on the floor.

When I looked further, to figure out how it got there, I witnessed a body of water receding from it. It rolled across the floor, with the same living consciousness as before!

Its path led to Jnfr, whose back was turned to me. From behind she resembled one of the Ntchru Nebu when they took on a human form.

*But her demeanor has changed. The feeling of loss that overcame her before is not present.*

I walked toward her while putting my suit on. When the suctions entered my pores, the sensation was not as bothersome as before.

Traces of blood were smeared across the floor, some of it from the battle earlier on and the rest was fresh, in the shape of footprints. I came to Jnfr's side and looked up at her face. She was entranced by the pool in front of her. There was a small puddle of blood surrounding her feet.

"The water is the blood of our home." she blurted, then turned to me and smiled. "That blood can cleanse much more than hearts."

We faced the pool for some time before she moved again, during that time the hue of the water shifted between spectrums more than a dozen times. She turned to face me again, her eyes pulsing with a violet light. Because it was almost pitch black in the room, the pulsing made it look as if her head was radiating with a bright aura.

Jnfr raised her arms and the water rose as well. She spread her fingers and the water spread out in finger-like projectiles. She began to move her arms about with the same elegance as her mother.

The water seemed linked to her movement and followed along. They danced together creating a series of postures that resembled the cosmic forms of the Ntchru.

Jnfr's breath matched the releasing and assuming of different positions, each time actually generating and dispersing the energy of whatever form she took.

The low mood that engulfed the entire room in a depressive state, began to lift as energetic waves reverberated through the room.

*This world must have some relation to my homeworld. Ta. Earth. The similarities between our spiritual practices are uncanny.*

I had visited many worlds that used motion and breathing to synergize with the nature around them. Yet there were few that shared the same approach of my culture.

As she continued, the watery mass slowly formed a duplicate body of Jnfr. I could see currents being exchanged through its feet and the surface of the pool. It towered over the both of us. Jnfr stopped her dance and looked to me smiling once more.

*She's still a child at heart, and that's good, her maturity should not be rushed regardless of extreme circumstances.*

I found that the watery doppelganger had a mind of its own, and ability to express it. It faced the both of us with its arms folded, and dripping: tapping its foot on the surface of the pool. It wanted to continue with its task.

Jnfr held her hand up, motioning for it to wait. "Most homes on this world are programmed by Tkkn and the surrounding air about the house."

"The program is designed to manage the house's upkeep and energy needs. You can call her...Mu."

She turned her head slightly to talk to me while maintaining her focus with the water. "Mother being very in tune with the All Nature, decided to program the house using water."

Jnfr paused then continued. "She figured that since the majority of our bodies were made of water, it would be easier to command."

*Impressive.*

*Past worlds that I have sojourned on used metal constructs, geared filled machines and elaborate electrical systems to accomplish their daily tasks.*

*This is the first time in ages, that I've seen beings that are genetically equivalent to me and utilizes the synergy with nature as a technology.*

In battle, I prefered to harmonize with the forces of nature to be victorious. But, when it comes to weaponry, whatever accomplishes the goal is the rule.

The impact and efficiency of a well placed laser gun blast is effortless, compared to driving steel into flesh and organs—*n*ot as satisfying, but so much more useful.

I prefered to save the devastation caused by my Ra blast or sekhem shout for circumstances that went beyond physical combat. Besides, they tended to leave my body depleted of all its stores, and at that point drawing upon raw sekhem could force me out my Khat.

Jnfr opened her mouth and exhaled a beautiful note. At first, it was in middle *c* and then rose higher in octave. The vibrations from her voice resonated throughout the room.

The sound was sweet to my ears... the waves of the melody brought forth memories of my childhood. Not only did the waves bring about a change in my mood, it also cleansed the mood of the room.

The murky vibrations, that blanketed the room and all the objects within it, began to break apart from its aggregation.

While I watched intensely the change that came about the room, I neglected to pay attention to the fact that I was gritting my teeth the whole time—that my fists shook and beads of sweat mixed in with the all my exposed extremities. I usually do this when I my spirit is aroused for battle, not a fight, but the possibilty of one.

*There was no battle, no real threat. What is this feeling? Justice. Her song sparks the feeling of justice; the kind felt when one is victorious for sake of others.*

My toes curled in, gripping the floor and my heartbeat raced. I found myself, without voluntary control, leaned towards Jnfr.

Without warning, the watery doppelganger of Jnfr, lashed out at me. It swung its arm at me with speed and force.

I know that it moved with enormous speed because I felt the fresh moist breeze that preceded it. I sensed it as I would experience the fresh air around a waterfall, except the impact had not taken place.

Amongst all this mental chatter, I landed safely on my feet after avoiding it. I crouched down and barred my teeth. As I turned my head, a slight breeze first hit my ear and then my cheek. Once I turned fully around, I saw that torn timber and other building materials had been pushed through a wall.

"Now we have to repair that as well. Damn idiot! Did you forget already that you cleansed her?" Jnfr scolded it. It hung its watery head down.

I do not think it forgot who I was, I think it sensed my battle spirit and thought I might harm Jnfr. It was protecting her.

Once she stopped to reprimand it, discontinuing her song, I returned to normal. I stood upright, keeping a watchful eye on her defender. I watched it behave as a young child would when their parent was disappointed.

Looking at the exchange between the two, I wondered how I moved so quick without leaving it and then taking an offensive stance. Had things progressed, I would have attacked Jnfr within a heartbeat, since she was the one in control of the threat.

"Go on!" Jnfr shouted at it.

It walked over the surface of the pool closer to me, knelt on one knee and held its hands out palms up. It bowed its head: it was apologizing!

"I accept." I gestured for it to rise.

Jnfr rubbed her eyes and yawned. "Let's finish this."

She stretched her arms out and yawned again. Then she resumed her song and movement.

After a series of postures and octaves, she turned to me.

"Let's get something to eat and rest. C'mon."

"What about here? Shouldn't we clean up this mess?"

"No. What do you think I was doing all that dancing and singing for? Mu will handle it. Let's eat!!"

I shrugged my shoulders and followed Jnfr out the room. My curiosity urged me stop and look back from behind the flaps.

Interesting.

Watery arms shot from out the canals, and collected the broken pieces of wood littered about. It pulled the pieces along the canal and into its water body. It drew the all the pieces into its torso area and started to spin them in several whirlpools.

At first I heard a low whirring sound which gradually progressed into high pitch and even higher pitch murmur. Eventually, the debris started to glow— more than likely from the heat that was being generated from its revolutions.

I could feel the heat radiate to where I was standing, followed by a small breeze. I enhanced my vision and saw that it extracted the stagnant emotions and energies impressed upon the wood.

The murky brown streams of vapor were pulled out the fibers of the wood that they clung onto. It was cleansing the debris from everything that soaked into it from the battle.

As I peered further, I realized that it also removed the heavy dust. This dust loated freely about the spaces between the smaller spheres that formed the cells of the fibers.

"I am hungry!" Jnfr tugged at my shoulder, I shooed her away.

The heavy dust cast thin webbings around the spheres as it moved past them, yet the extraction removed those webbings and withered them away.

Once everything was done, the rapid spinning of the whilrpools ceased and left several amber hue globes floating in the lower part of its body. In the upper-part of its body, dark brown unstable looking globes circled about.

Without warning, it squatted and drew in its bent arms until its elbows touched its sides. Tremors from the tension generated by the posture rippled across the surface of the pool.

The shockwaves rumbled across the floor and reached where I stood. Abruptly, it rose up and threw its arms into the air, the unstable energy in its body shot out its palms in a stream of globular energy. Rather than hitting the face of the ceiling, it veered from it, as if consciously seeking release from the room.

It found it in the hole that it was in, some sense, a sibling to. Although, I wanted to continue to observe, I followed Jnfr upstairs.

Her disposition shifted back and forth at a whim. I wondered if her behavior was a result of the traumatic events— or something else.

# N

## *Chapter Medju Fedu*
## *Fight*

*When is Jnfr coming back to the city?*

*I want to hold her again and get closer.* I was almost there yesterday. I almost had her.

*Hmmm. Maybe the timing was off. Yeah, bad timing and poor location.*

But I just couldn't help myself, she smelled so good! That scent that comes off her body made me so hot—I could literally feel myself driving deep inside of her until we were united.

Yeah, like that was going to happen in an alley after her mother just finished beating that Rkm boy up.

Besides if we did unite, she would know all about my dealings with her father. Before I could settle with them, she would get in the way of things.

*Just two more matches to go. Two. Sigh.*

*Well, let me get off these streets, its still early and some of the losers from last night may just be waking up out their stupors. And I need more of a peace of mind rather than the exercise I would get from tossing them around.*

I hesitated before I pushed the doors of The Hold and got bombarded by the musky stench of men combined with liquor smells from bottles and on people's breath.

*I hate this place.*

My nose hairs burned as I adjusted my eyes to the dim lights spread about the room.

This place could use some incense and serious mop downs. Are they open to make a profit? Or just as an unofficial clubhouse for The Fever carriers?

*What patron wants to walk on bloodstained floors for a drink?*

I walked past the bartender, who was hard at work cleaning glasses or at least making sure that the spots weren't too visible.

*Damn, how about using some hot water for once? Maybe you would get more patrons.*

But, The Hold wasn't so much for patrons as it was for those with The Fever. I nodded at him as I always did, and he scrunched up his face as he always did.

Not my fault he bets on losers. He should stop focusing on taking their tkkn with drinks before they fought, maybe they would stand more of a chance sober in the ring.

*Not that it would matter. Most of them have the Fever and it clouds their senses. Makes them very predictable. The only two who I would have difficulty with is Dvln and Jnfr's father, Drrn.*

I'd seen them in action, they were so close to bursting and expiring, that they were forced to learn to control their reactions.

"What the hell man! Clean this damn blood up off the floor!" I yelled out. I just couldn't take the mess anymore. "I'm tired of coming in this bitch and almost busting my head from slipping on blood!"

When I finished, some big guy charged at me and wrapped his hands around my neck. I allowed it. I was mad and needed to blow off some steam.

Before the pressure of his fingers pushed into my throat, I pinched his nose with a quick burst of strength then snatched away.

When he let go of my neck and went to hold his face, I punched him in the solar plexus as hard as I could. I sent out most of my anger in the form of a pressure blast through my fist. I heard some vertebrae snap before he fell flat to the floor.

*Think I went a little too far.*

"Ah... clean up this mess too." I felt much better leaving that fool sprawled out in the puddle I'd slipped on.

I caught a glimpse of Drrn sitting in the far off corner, he was preoccupied with something and didn't notice my little squabble. There was barely any light there except for something that kept glowing bright then dim.

"Hi Kvn... Drrn has very good control of it." When Rkm spoke, his words shook me from thinking of Jnfr.

"He can take the power needed and control the rising of The Fever. I witnessed him put his entire arm through someone's body without breaking a sweat." Rkm finished nervously, like Drrn could read his lips from where he sat.

Drrn always ended things with intimidation or extreme violence, one or the other.

*Come to think of it, I've never saw him do more than just one move. I guess that's all it takes to finish someone when you can impale them with your arm.*

A barmaid came over to us with a plate of food. Fried wings and baked tubers. I can hardly eat this type of mess myself.

In fact this type of food is a favorite of those with The

Fever. The average person would be physically unable to digest such a combination, their bodies would not allow it to be brought to their mouths. Besides, most of the time the meat was filled with angry energy from the animal it was taken from.

"Want some?" Rkm offered, looking at me with a mouthful of wings in his mouth.

"Nah, enjoy yourself." I pushed the plate back to him.

He shrugged his shoulders and continued to gorge himself. I had to move away from him, the combination of the smell of his food, and the overall stench of the bar made my stomach turn. I got up, beat the side of my chest to show respect and then walked toward Drrn.

*Poor Rkm. He's caught up in all this mess of his father's and Drrn's. He's not built for this lifestyle.*

Drrn did something to what he was holding and the corner he sat at became dark. As I got closer to him, I noticed a tense mist in the air becoming thicker.

Was it The Fever or the heat Drrn was shedding off? Whatever it was, my skin and eyes burned when it came into contact with the mist that hung in the air. I'd felt this before when I came to see him, although this time it was becoming unbearable.

By the time I sat down in front of him, my eyes were

already tearing and I was scratching my skin.

"Wipe your face, Kvn. You look a mess."

He handed me a cloth, that looked like it already had been raked across someone's dirty sweaty face. Brown and yellow stains were all over it. At first I thought they were creases in it because of the lack of light.

He still motioned it toward me to take it.

"I am not using that," I said. "I'll be fine."

I pushed his hand away, but in the back of my mind I thought of Rkn's story about the "arm through the body."

"Be a mess then," he said, like he could care less. But he cared more than what he was showing.

Drrn tossed the dirt rag away and sucked his teeth. He was annoyed. "Down to business."

*Here it comes.*

"Last night, you did well…almost too well."

"In what way?" I answered like I didn't know.

"You took out my competition with ease. No deaths. And you made sure that they wouldn't be fighting anymore."

"But—" This is not the first time I'd heard this.

"You also took a few of my guys down…permanently"

"Drrn, you told me to fight for your side so that I can get what I want. I've done that."

"You have," he said, tight-lipped.

"Well, I can't help it if your guys walk around throwing their intent at me and then trying to carry it out— only to be broken up in the end."

"Broken up is fine. Dead, I have a problem with. I can't use them when they are the next realm. I tried…the All Nature doesn't allow that."

"I can't switch this thing off and on. It is my natural trained reaction to want to stay alive…by any means."
I continued, although I knew I was putting myself deeper in danger. "Your guys hurt people, sometimes kill them. If I get killed by them before the finish of our contract. What then?"

Drrn inhaled deeply and then grunted. He placed both his hands on the table, rolling them back and forth along the surface; then slouched back in his seat.

"You know. It's pain in the asses like you who make me loose my cool. I mean really lose it." He sighed deeply. "Alright. Watch yourself. You are done here…for now." He finished, not looking at me, shooing me away and continuing his focus on his toy.

I walked away feeling a little weak..scared. Like I was warned by him in such a way that I was put at a disadvantage. He'd made it clear that his men could not be sent to the next realm by me.

Problem is, they will definitely attempt to send me to the next realm, now more than ever. Something about the way I am pisses them off, gives them an attitude.

*Did Drrn really openly give his consent for open-season on me? Did he?*

*I'm sure he did. They would come at me harder than ever. And when we start getting physical, neither one of us will stop.*

While passing through the bar, I attempted not to show anything physically or energetically fearful. It was difficult. I kept my wits about me, watching the figures who shifted about the shadows, moving against the walls and sitting at tables they didn't start at.

I knew I could handle anything they came at me with. My worry— my fear— was my father's safely, and what Drrn might do to him. These fools running about were trying to irk me, so that I would make a mistake.

And their scent was changing, becoming more hostile as I walked toward the door.

"Catch!" a mug was thrown at me from the shadows, followed by another.

I moved out the way with ease. Unfortunately, they kept on going and smashed two guys in the face. They stood up quick and scraped off chips of the mug stuck in their skin, tearing away at their own flesh.

This is the part that always was both hilarious and yet sad to me. Instead of finding out who really caused their bloody faces, they gave in to anger and grabbed anyone who was close to them.

Which is usually when I'm around.

A split second before they pushed their feet into the floor to lunge at me, I looked at Drrn. He was looking at me the whole time. Expressionless. Still tinkering with his toy, but definitely fixed on me.

Just then, all the lights went out in the bar. The bartender must have shut them off through his connection with the main tekken board.

I saw him glaring at me through the darkened room. He smiled ear to ear, while looking for his club under the bar counter.

*Drrn wants me dead, I know that now. My usefulness to him is done. I know…I know that's what he is thinking. My father…will suffer the same fate.*

At first my thoughts ran wild in my head, but I quieted them quick as I could. As I calmed my heart's thumping, I ignored the tugs at the top of my shirt by one the guys with a bleeding face.

I also paid no attention to the remarks and slanders that came with the shaking. I relaxed and let my body go loose as it shook back it forth.

What I *did* pay attention to was the collective rising scent and heat of The Fever in the air...along with the air currents of the folks creeping up slowly behind me.

One of them was inching up a little slower than the other, shifting his weight side to side. I could sense one of his arms doing the same.

*From his movement, I'm sure he's carrying some type of weapon; keeping himself ready to strike from any position and at any moment.*

What little light that shone through the dirty ass windows of the bar, only allowed me to see the shadows of those who were surrounding me. When dude shook me once more, I allowed the momentum to carry my body forward and dropped an open palm on his nose.

He bent forward grunting and tried to hold his face with both hands. I kept his hand pinned to me when he tried to let go.

*I can't believe this guy actually just whimpered in pain!*

While whatever self-pity he had kept him occupied, I pivoted my body and stepped forward—causing him to fly over the table and into my personal stalker creeping up from behind. Their heads collided knocking them both out.

The bottle the stalker guy had fell out his hands and sounded like it broke into three pieces. I stomped and grinded against their hands; immediately crushing the small bones in them.

*Now usually this sound really bothers me but seeing they are knocked out, at least I won't hear any complaints from them.*

I made sure everyone else heard their bones grinding underneath my foot, it caused those in the shadows to pause for a bit. They gasped and their feet tripped up, as I rolled my foot back and forth on a mangled hand. I bellowed out in laughter—something I never did when handling these guys.

I wanted to be uncharacteristic in my behavior, make them think they were dealing with someone who not only was their better in combat, but now was beginning to go mad.

The person that was still behind the table, who smelled worst than his partner, drew back from me confused. He then dropped his head, and sluggishly dove at me, still a little shaken up from the mug smashing into his face.

I quickly judged where one of those pieces of glass might have landed, snatched one up from the ground and drove it deep in between his shoulder blades.

He suddenly jerked out of his forward movement and tried to reach it to pull it out. He couldn't. As he hunched over struggling to reach it, I brought my elbow down on the back of his neck.

He fell to my feet unconscious. A spark flew out a tkkn from one of the corners then the lights came on. It took only a second to see I was surrounded. Two large men blocked the exit door while others encircled me, inching up little by little. At least the bodies laid out in front of me made it difficult to rush at me.

"During this little outburst, have you thought once about your father?" Drrn called from out of the crowd.

He slowly walked out from them with his left arm outstretched in back of him, dragging something along… my father.

Drrn dropped my father's limp arm—his hand hit the floor lifelessly.

My heart jumped into my throat, I couldn't breathe. I started to lean forward to leap at Drrn, I couldn't help myself. Drrn lifted his head and caught wind of the offensive energy that came off my body. He relaxed his muscles, ready to attack me first.

I stopped myself right before I gathered skhm into my legs

and feet and contracted my muscles to the point of tearing.

"I have grown weary of you." Drrn's voice carried no feeling, yet was resoundingly deep. "Very, *very* weary. Coming in here like some Golden Child of the All Nature."

He cupped his hand to his ear. "Any smart shit to say now? Perception is something else, isn't it?"

Then he cleared his throat. "*This* is what we are going to do."

I relaxed and listened, while keeping an eye on his face for the slightest sign of muscle tension. *I will not rush into death—especially since I don't know whether or not my father is still alive.*

"You will have one last match instead of two. Just one. In this match you will not only defeat your opponent, you will kill him and then…his leader."

*Kill? I will kill you for what you did to my father!*

"Or you can die. You and your father, here and now." He scratched his head. "In fact, I am leaning more to having the both of you killed now." The heat is the room fluxed for a brief moment but I didn't care.

"But," Drrn continued, "I need that leader dead more than I need you to be."

He swiftly cocked his leg back and kicked my father's side, lifting his body up into the air and sending it flying towards me.

When his feeble body struck mine, I almost fell to pieces, as I dropped to my knees to catch him before he hit the floor.

*He's alive…barely. Very close to transition and now that I finally have him back, there is little I can do for him.*

I held him close, my hug nearly squeezed what little life was left in him.

“Kvn... Do not worry yourself over me.” the rasping of my father's voice tore at my heart.

“This is not,” *cough cough* “how I raised you...this is not what I want to see.”

“Father...I...” I could not speak. No words left my lips. Fear and weakness overcame me. All I could do to avoid shaking was be silent. But everyone in the bar knew. Everyone.

A strong wave of heat swept across the room. The air along with the spirit pressure pushed against thewalls and left dents in the wood. The remaining drunkards at the bar stumbled out their stools, trying to get a grasp of their equilibrium, but then dropped to the floor.

I shielded my father's body at the risk of exposing my back to the mob. When I turned away from them, I felt the force of their intentions ripping at my back in flurries. The air pressure and the waves of their primal selves, almost worked in unison to make that force feel like actual attacks.

*"Now..."* my father's whisper barely reached my ears.

Most of my attention was taken by the moment when physical contact would be initiated. All I wanted was for my father's final days to be peaceful. But my body's shielding his, gave little hope for that.

I looked back at Drrn. "I did what you wanted. Kept the strength of your clique much stronger than its own members."

Drrn looked down at me smirking. "So." his response was as cold as his breath, it felt like ice when it reached my face. "Yes or no?"

*"No."* crept out of father's dried mouth.

All of sudden his body tensed up below me, and then gradually filled with vitality and muscular tone. His dried flesh became invigorated with blood and spiritual pressure. A pulse of energy shot out from his body and into mine.

Drrn's men scrunched up their faces and moved about uneasily.

*It could be in reaction to the change in atmosphere around father.*

Breathing became difficult for me because of the increase of heat and musk escaping from their bodies. Growling and hissing grew slowly in their ranks... all of which Drrn put in check with a long glance at all of them.

They stopped immediately and shook in the stances doing their best to repress their natural feelings. But that wouldn't last for long. Father's definitive "No" was heard by everyone, and all of them waited for me to speak.

I looked at them all, especially Drrn and shook my head side to side. "No."

Then, I found myself doing something I never did in combat. I prepared to brace for the attack. I sprawled out over father and tightened my muscles. I dug my feet into the wood floor along with my knees and hands, looking for any way to get traction.

*This is it…my war is over.*

At least I could grant my father and myself a few more moments…together. My eyes started to burn from the toxins in the air and fearful thoughts in my head. Tears poured out my eyes. I wanted to rub them but I just let them fall on father rather than risk changing my position.

The first strike was heavy and came at my shoulder. The weight of it tore into it me, the way a beast would, pulling out flesh as it retracted. I arched back in agony, nearly bit off a piece of my tongue holding in my yells. When I dropped to the floor my hands flew out to catch my balance and avoid crushing father.

Claws— not nails—ripped into me. *The fever is changing the bodies of these men for the worst. Which makes it worst for me.*

Another came at me, swung so wildly that it completely missed me, sending the air it dragged with it to strike my body. My body stood firm, while the air coldly hit my open wound and caused me a little panic.

More than panic. For the first time I feared for my life, and not like before, I actually felt the death coat my tongue. In all the fights I ever had, I never by choice chose not to fight and I never been wounded too seriously.

As blood ran down my arm, my resolve grew weak. I closed my eyes and held my father even tighter— trembling in anticipation of the next attack.

"Scared? Maybe you will join us. Fear of death is what gave birth to our little bar club." Drrn spoke with joy and smiled widely, bloodthirsty intent came in his voice.

I continued to stay in my one position. A shell. Only a small part about me stayed hopeful, when I was able to look father in the eyes. I sensed the air-pressure change around me again, someone had just cocked back their arm and was synergizing the air with it.

They are starting to get smarter and deadlier. My whole body flinched from the feel of the attack, contacting the hairs

on my head. I closed my eyes tight and embraced my father who struggled to get
free of me.

*That's right, I forgot…we fight to the end.*

The attacker sent his arm towards me. The sekhem projected from it was aimed at my lower back. *The velocity and weight of it will do more than puncture my kidneys.*

He swung, connected and I remained unharmed. He struck but I felt nothing. My father slapped me real hard. Although I felt like lead just sat on my face I still kept my eyes open and looked over my shoulder. I jerked back from what I saw. Two huge men viciously swung at my back screaming wildly.

But, every attack repelled back at them by something unseen. Eventually I became aware of the barrier that my father created, utilizing the natural shield that hovered over his skin. All he did was extend it out further than his body and used his life-force to strengthen it.

Seeing their attacks were ineffective only made them become more vicious and heavier with force.

Eventually that would cause them irreparable damage in their joints and tendons. Each time their attacks struck, bones cracked quietly under the pounded flesh that muffled it.

And they kept at it…until Drrn bared his teeth which seemed to make them docile. With dazed looks on their faces, they heaved at the chest and staggered, swinging their dislocated battered arms as if in trance.

Drrn's left eye began to twitch.

"Prepare for my eye." Father spoke with newly regained strength.

He had been watching me watch them. I looked down at him, he was restored to full health and vitality. His thick lips formed a line, no expression.

I nodded. A tingling sensation ran through my body followed by a coolness passing through every cell. He reached out for me and caught hold of my arms.

Then…I sensed Drrn in rage, his sekhem was becoming unstable. The air pressure imposed on father's barrier became denser— heavier. I looked back at him taking my focus off father and disrupting his link with me.

Drrn knocked the two men out his way and started to wail savagely on the surface. He continued on increasing in strength and speed.

The Fever had him now. He grunted and roared from the pit of his being— fixated on getting to us to rip us apart. It didn't take long for blood to form like a dome over us from the repeated attacks.

"Kvn!" Father called out to me.

When I turned my attention to him, I saw that he had been silently melding with me. My arms were covered in his flesh that slowly crept up to my shoulders. Why was he doing it this way?

"Why father?! Why *this* way?" I bellowed.

At first he was silent, the expression on his face grim. "I cannot take my spirit form. I can only manipulate my flesh but so far." He paused. "And only in this way."

Father looked away then back at me, directly into my eyes. "Please do your best to accept how I am passing my eyes to you…do your best to comprehend," he finished letting out a gasp.

His final breath in this world passed into the realm next to this one, not to return….until I bring a son into this world.

I pulled myself from the grief that was entering my lungs and brought my attention to the immediate threat. Drrn.

He continued his onslaught behind the now blood drenched barrier, I could only imagine his current state behind that wall. Even with my father's eye, it would be a real fight… one with lost of limb and deep wounds.

I looked down at father's lifeless body. Although his eyes stared right back at me still retaining life, when I moved my arm, I felt his flesh bounded to me— skin that I dare not peel off.

Blood and other energies were still coursing from his body into mine; yet, his soul had departed leaving some of his essence in his life fluid. Suddenly the eyes began to rotate around then bulge out, pushing forward until they were free of the sockets.

The nerves and vessels attached to them snapped and leaked fluids. I almost got sick from the sight. Next, they rolled down his cheeks then along his neck and onto his shoulders leaving a light trail behind them.

I kept still and quiet, filled with anger...intermingled with grief. *It's hard for me to accept that things have escalated so fast within but a small passing of moments.*

*But here I am, underneath a dome, shielded from men who want me dead…with no chance of rebirth. I just don't know anymore.*

*Eye or no eye, I just don't know. And what's worst, is that the constant battering of Drrn's fist sounding like a shallow drumbeat, is the only thing I find solace in.*

The deadening sounds were constant and ironically the only thing that I could count on that was stable. Its rhythm almost lulled me to sleep despite everything taking place.

Meanwhile, the eyes continued to make their way towards

me, slowly rolling off his arms and into mine.

Once they got to my face, anxiety set in and my first response was to yank them off, but I steadied myself. The moisture feeling across my cheeks sent shivers down my spine and once they stopped they were literally eye to eye with my own.

I kept re-focusing to avoid straining my eyes and to be able to keep them open. They started to push into my eyes, the pressure was maddening and painful. Once they could not force their way anymore, they began to dissolve into them. My vision continued to get blurry.

As it felt like the remaining parts were being absorbed, total darkness came with it. No light of any kind— not even from my thoughts. I went to touch my eyes with my hands, but I could not move them.

*I can't move! This is not right! It was not supposed to be this way. Father pushed himself to transition and passing the eye before he was fully prepared .*

*What's going to happen next? How long will I be in this darkness? I literally feel nothing.*

*Nothing for my emotions to attach themselves to. No rapid beating of my heart. No pressure in my head or from the outside on my skin. Nothing.*

Then a slight tingling in my head began to grow. From tingling to pain then to agony. I was now able to move my arms but I still couldn't see. I rolled my body over and came to my knees.

When I tried to push myself up, someone kicked me back down. I came to my knees again this time anticipating the move to push me back down and was able to stand up fully.

My senses slowly returned to me, the stench of the room was the first thing to hit me, so strong that I almost threw up. Then vision followed almost instanouesly.

"You are going to die! Right *here* and right *now!*" Drrn yelled.

His usually calm demeanor had been replaced with hostility. He had been beating me while I was paralyzed. I was unable to avoid his next swin and my head went whipping back catching the view of the entire room on the way.

I saw with shock that father's body was gone without a trace!

"Looking for your father? My men ate him when that pitiful barrier broke." Drrn was taunting me— although I wouldn't put it pass his men to do something like that.

I staggered back trying to buy myself enough time to get my head together. Drrn was not about to afford such a luxury.

He came galloping across the wood floor, sending dents into it as he rushed at me. He plowed his fist into the upper right side of my chest.

Ribs cracked and flesh tore over his arm as he kept on driving it in deeper. Drrn fiendishly groped around my insides and located my liver. He caught a tight grip on it and squeezed, blood gushed onto his arm from the rupturing of vessels.

Excrutiaing pain slammed into my body followed by numbness. My neck reeled back, while I beat wildly on his arm to get free.

He brought his lips to my ear. "Where is all that arrogance now? Let me guess. No one has gotten this close to you before." He squeezed tighter. "*Have* they?"

He continued to steadily wring at my organ however, it did not give way to the pressure and acted more like a sponge.

Still the pain was unbearable. I looked everywhere around the room I could just to keep from looking into his eyes.

But the sights were not encouraging. Only eyes filled with contempt and madness, fists beating into palms and large bodies further engorged with blood and skhm.

And then my eyes met Rkm's, they lacked life and his complexion was almost grey. We were trapped in each other's stare for a few moments before he turned away.

I began to feel faint. My eyelids grew heavy, couldn't remain conscious for too much longer. Drrn head-butted the shit out of my eye... then something happened.

I felt a stirring in me. I wanted to live.

"Changing your mind about giving up?" Drrn said sarcastically. "I found that a well-placed headbutt either knocks someone out or revives them—makes them riled up."

He clutched my liver into his palm while more of my life fluid spilled out on the both of us. At this point, I was pretty much numb and pain just became a dull sensation.

"I'm glad to see you decided to stick around for a bit longer. This wouldn't be as enjoyable if you didn't."

I could care less about anything he thought. Whatever stirred inside of me was now seeking to be let out. I caused my liver to secrete an acid from the fresh and newly created membrane around it. Drrn's grip lessened and was replaced by cooling energy.

*He must be trying to resist with some type of coolant excreted from his own skin.*

It didn't matter, the corrosive nature of my acid quickly adapted and bored through whatever defenses he had. While his attention was on countering, I sharply yanked his arm from out of me—almost losing consciousness from the pain.

A glob of blood plopped out revealing his hand dissolved to the bone. The sound of his hand sizziling didn't seem to take away from his disposition. Neither did the blood that splattered on his foot which began to dissolve it. He swung with his other hand for my jaw— the force of if would take my jaw clean off, if it connected.

I dropped to the height of his chin, and moved towards that side of his body. Seeing what I was planning to do, he tried to switch up his movement. He left his side open, and I took what he gave me— my thumb thrusted deep under his armpit.

Looking past his body I saw his men's expressions change, some tapped each other on the shoulder and started over to us.

"You are a smart S.O.B. Enjoy the time you still have alive." Drrn taunted, while his voice faded out.

He collapsed to the ground, no doubt The Fever was over-exerted by the sudden release of toxic fluids underneath the armpits.

The spiritual and air pressure about him, snapped out of its spiraling and the air became clear…or at least *clearer.* I figured this would be a good time as any to pop some mess and throw these fools off balance.

"You saw that, right?" I licked my lips and started pointing my finger at them, keeping my other hand closed over my wound. "Dropped him even with my gut torn open. What'll you think will happen to you?"

They froze up in their tracks.

"Make a hole and let me outta here."

Most of them did as I told them while others stood defiant. I glanced at the cocky ones and then smirked at them and rubbed my cheek.

I bent over Drrn's body and looked him over. He was snoring. *After all that, he actually just fell into a deep sleep.*

I drew my arm back and punched him as hard as I could without tearing the newly created flesh around my wound. His face swelled up, I spat on it and kicked him in his side.

The last of the men who opposed me nervously stood aside and cleared the way. I made my way through their gauntlet not avoiding one of their stares, hitting them right back with the same energy they gave me.

I very close to the exit, when someone bawled out. "If he was able to knock out Drrn, why wait for him to pick us off one by one?"

The mood of the bar instantly changed and the air pressure grew thick.

"We might as well swarm him now and kill him!" I recognized that voice. It was Rkm.

I rushed towards the exit as the level of charged hostility stagnated the air with its presence and stench. The gauntlet of fever enraged men closed in on me as a few rushed down the center of it at me.

I blacked-out. I don't know how many skulls I cracked and with what I did it with. All I knew that it wasn't enough —the bar was filled with more of their members than I figured on.

My strength was waning. "Get him! He's weak!" Rkm screamed out from across the room.

I often heard that a sheep will become like a wolf at the sight of blood. *This sheep needs to shut his trap up!*

I dashed in his direction, pivoting, sidestepping and barreling over crazed men. Once I got to him, I grabbed him by the neck, he trembled in my grasp just before the deadening slap to his shoulder.

He clumsily staggered back into some men charging at me—his shoulder bulged out from the pressure building in it. I pulled out my firestick and shot it at him just as his arm exploded.

The minature creatures that inhabited his body were highly volatile when exposed to heat. I knew that from Jnfr.

He and the others around him burst into flame—stumbling about setting everything else aflame that they touched. Finally, I had an opportunity while everyone was paying more attention to the blaze that rapidly spread across the bar.

Ever since I received father's eye, I had been sifting through the imprinted information stored in the cells of blood, cones and rods. Individual images of intricate geometric shapes were spread all about with no instructions on how they related to one another.

*Wait. Mr-K-B.* Mrkb... that's the sound of the word that came about when I finally arranged the shapes so they would fit into one another. I recall father mentioning that a Mrkb was the key to entering the Folds of The All-Nature. Ironic that on that same day, his was snatched away by Drrn.

The flames spread quickly, there was almost no way I could get to the exit safely. Noticing that the Bar Counter was not engulfed in flames, I rushed over and leapt behind it. After landing on the axphisiated body of the bartender and kicking it away from me, I quickly soaked a towel, that was hanging from a rack, in water.

I wrapped it around my nose and mouth then fanned away the thick black smoke that slowly surrounded me.

There was no time to waste, I had to do whatever I thought would work. I focused my breath and pulled the images into my heart... *Skhm Shn Ra*... it just felt like the natural thing to do.

Something tore at the space in front of me, sucking in the air around me.

A small dark portal opened up.

I dove in without a second thought.

## *Chapter Medju Deyu*
## *Family*

While Jnfr prepared the meal, Mu kept reaching for the spoon she was stirring with, looking to be helpful. She was already annoyed about having to throw out the soup she made earlier.

Jnfr mentioned to me, as she poured it out into the sink, that the potency of it quickly turns rancid after being left out in the open and unattended.

Mu did not let up, it glided over to the ingredients that needed preparation, but Jnfr shoved it away from the cutting board. It tried again—not minding the spoon being swatted at it, allowing some strikes to pass in and out.

Jnfr's face grew intense. The floor vibrated where she stood and sent a minor tremor throughout the house. She sighed deeply, then washed the spoon thoroughly.

*I guess the water from the faucet and Mu are not one in the same.*

"Go finish the repair of the floor and leave me alone!" Jnfr scolded.

Mu left and then returned in a moments. It sprinkled a few drops on Jnfr's face.

"Okay, okay I see you repaired everything. Now please just leave me alone to cook." Jnfr's voice was starting to sound strained. There was sadness in her words, and she trembled as she stirred the soup.

"You should be grateful I am letting you out for this long." Her words whipped out at Mu when she swung her neck around. Mu retracted back and dropped its head.

"Fine!" Jnfr said. "Go cut those over there."

Mu happily glided over to the cutting board filled with leafy green vegetables. It grabbed a bunch up and laid them out straight to be cut. A blade formed from its hand. Just when Mu was about to cut, Jnfr interceded.

"Make sure you use the metal blade next to it, not your own. That blade is attuned to the vegetables so they won't be putting up any sort of fight when you part them."

Jnfr grunted...and the area where I sat tremored a little.

"That's why I don't let you in the kitchen, you always

forget important details like that." She continued her verbal abuse. "You sure are a miserable Hn! Hand me the leaves after you are done." She finished leaving a lingering breathe of disgust in the air.

Mu hunched over slowly and trembled then set to work with its new orders. Once done it meekly handed the leaves to Jnfr. Jnfr snatched them away and feverently washed them.

Mu slowly gathered up the stalks and absorbed the water out of them. Then it took the stringy fibers left into its form, and molded them into a patch of the floor that was discolored. The way Mu held its form gave off the impression of it being embarrassed…ashamed like child.

I watched their whole interaction from the same seat I had when I first arrived at their household—making use of the yarn and needles, Jnfr gave me to keep myself occupied.

Joy filled my heart to be able to relax and use my fingers, for something other than sending adversaries to the Duat. Knitting was my first love so many eons ago.

At first as a simple hobby, and providing clothing for my family. As war times approached, my skill was used for knitting chainmail. Then the needle became a hammer, and I began to work metal for armor.

Finally I drew a sword when my family was threatened—

leaving the knitting needles to collect dust. Now, as I watched my fingers work the needles into the yarn. I began to hum, comforted by the vibration of my lips, a sensation they have long forgotten.

And then it struck me, I had just experienced a dramatic turn in my life, without suffering from depression. Or a need to run away... or create an alter-ego. Mu's shifting of its hips, and waving of its arms to the rhythm of my humming quickly cut short my contemplation.

Jnfr held her stomach as she giggled from laughter. "That's enough from you," she spoke up loudly. "Go back." She shooed Mu away.

Mu fell to the floor, loosing the humanoid form it took, and seeped into the wood before it could collect as a pool. I turned my attention back to my work. I wanted to make some type of wrap skirt.

*My battle-suit may appear a little out of place with this world's clothing style. No need to draw attention. As it is, my stature already does that for me since everyone on this planet are giants in comparison.*

*I might be able to pass for a child but no one would believe that with the fullness of my figure— especially the fullness of my breasts.*

Jnfr looked at me. "What are you working on?"

"I am thinking about some type of wrap skirt."

"Oh." She paused. "I have something like that, would you like to see it for the pattern?"

"Yes."

She stopped what she was doing in the kitchen and whispered some words over the pot before covering it. "That'll be alright on its own for a bit... Be right back."

She slipped behind some screens and later came back with a simple wrap skirt. "Here..." She handed it to me.

The material was different than the yarn she'd given me. It seemed to dissolve into my skin at the touch. In any case, my innate skill for working material picked up on the pattern quickly and I set to work.

My hands moved rapidly as the information from my memories fed my hands with all that I needed to construct what I wanted. *All I need is a loom…and some more yarn.*

Jnfr looked at me puzzled. "I would never have pegged you for someone who would be into this." She scratched her head. "You'll never be able to create it going about it that way."

She took what was left of the yarn and the dress from me. "Place it out like this." She laid the dress out on the floor.

*I don't see what is so special about she did it.*

"Now take the yarn in your hand and roll it over the material, with the intention to create."

I did as she said and rolled the ball over the dress. Gradually, images began entered my mind, showing the step by step construction of the dress. Along with the impression of the personal intention of the one who made the dress…Tzkw.

My eyes closed gently without responding to the need to focus inward. I saw every cross-pattern, weave and stitch however. I did not perceive the means by which it was done — only the material taking form. When I came back to the presence of the room and opened my eyes, they became fixed on the ball of yarn: now floating and glowing in mid-air in front of me. I held the needles tightly then let them slip out my hand.

"Do you see now?" Jnfr asked.

"Yes."

"OKay then. I am going back to cooking." She smiled at me, then stood up and walked back to the kitchen.

I innerstood clearly what she meant and got to work.

"Start." I spoke to the yarn.

Jnfr didn't have to tell me what to do. I just *knew* what to say, it came natural. And the yarn responded to my creative will, which seemed to combine with its own force to keep it levitating.

A mental jerk from it called for me to perform the next move... the tugging grew very irritating, as if it was impatient.

Then it dawned on me. I was missing a loom!

"Nth." Jnfr called across the room. "I forgot to tell you to choose the material for the loom. Air or Blood?"

"What?"

"Oh." She rubbed her head. "Since you are new to this, you are not able to read all the imprinted instructions on your consciousness."

"Your cells are not able to receive the next commands through their cell walls and your thoughts only realize their presence."

"I innerstand." I was relieved that despite her childish ways she was able to clarify the ways of her world.

"Good." She paused. "Air looms help you to construct quickly and make your garment extremely flexible but not durable. Blood is slow in construction but very strong in material."

"I see."

"Now the thing with blood is— " Before she finished, I issued the command for blood.

In response to my thought, a few strings darted at me and penetrated my hands. Even if I could move quick enough, their intentions would overcome me. It seemed linked to the information I absorbed earlier and injected what felt like fine thread-like tubes into my bloodstream.

It didn't cause me any pain; not that much could anyway. I looked towards Jnfr perplexed.

"You *did* say blood." She shrugged her shoulders and continued tending to the food. Her hand covered her lips, to hide her giggling.

Slowly my blood was drawn out leaving a tingling sensation through my palm as it pumped through. Meanwhile, the outer parts of the loom were formed and then finally the inner parts with my life-fluid.

Once the loom was finished, it withdrew its strings from my hands, leaving no sign of entering. The yarn strung itself into the loom, and started in on creating the pattern pieces of the dress I desired.

The front, back and ties were all crafted in a matter of minutes. I wondered how quick an air loom operates. With the pieces completed and the yarn all used up, the only thing left was to stitch it together.

Another mental tug. I see in my minds eye it was waiting for the command to stitch.

"Stitch."

In direct response to my words, the blood changed composition, becoming top snitch thread-like bundles. Without

the use of a needle it entered the fabric and
pulled the pieces together. With care and precision the
final parts were hemmed together until no parts of the
loom remained.

The finish product glided over to me through the air, and laid itself in my lap and rubbed itself along my thigh the way a pet would.

"Try it on." Jnfr motioned to me with her spoon.

I placed the dress aside, rose up out of the comfortable floor seats and stretched a little; some of my limbs were in need of movement. I looked at the dress, it was simple but well-made.

*I would have preferred dark blue.*

Bit by bit, the hue of the material altered itself and became the exact color I wanted. As I leaned over to pick it up, it jumped at me. Feeling no apprehension, I allowed it to wrap around by body and secure the ties.

"I guess it has a little of your fire." Jnfr chuckled.

"Looks like it does." I replied with a smile when it slightly squeezed my waist with something close to a hug.

Although the material looked like cloth, when I touched it, it had a more rubbery metallic feel. Similar to my suit. In fact, the fibers of the dress meshed into my suit or at least latch onto one another. Their contact created a pleasant heat, emitted all around my legs.

"The dress reflects its owner's personality in the texture of the material. Especially with the material you chose," Jnfr explained.

"Nth, excuse me for saying, but you have a great figure for someone that was so drenched with the smell of blood."

*Was that a compliment?*

"Our meal is finished. Just needs to cool." She placed the lid of the pot to the side.

She reached for a small blue statue of Heru that was next to a box of coals. She rested it across from the red-hot coals underneath the pot, brought her lips to the side of it and spoke a few words. Waves of heat slowly drew into the statute and shifted its hue from a bluish color to a fiery red.

"This takes too long. I still rather take them out with my hand." Jnfr said aloud.

Abruptly, she stopped moving and stood silently, becoming slowly out of sync with her surroundings. Next she walked backwards, her body convulsed with every step while her facial expression remained plain. Finally she turned about and walked towards the kitchen counter.

Jnfr slammed her hands on its surface and began to sob.

"Mother..." the words fell out her mouth faintly.

She pounded the counter. The shifting of her energy affected the entire room, setting the atmosphere of the room at *disease.*

I watched without saying a word or moving while she repeatedly lashed out at her immediate area. *This is wrong. This is not just grieving of a young girl. What has a hold on her?*

I looked deeper but only could detect waves of heat coursing around her. Then my left eye throbbed a little and with that throbbing came the ability to see that there was another being in the room with us.

A red etheric spirit.

It circled about her as she threw her tantrum— screaming and yelling all types of madness. The energy around her was similar to the one who attacked her mother and attributed to her transition.

Suddenly she turned to me, her face full of tears and strained expression. "This is your fault," she murmured.

"This is your fault," raising her voice and slamming the counter.

I said nothing.

"THIS IS YOUR FAULT!" she screamed at me.

At that point, the spirit forced its way into her brow then

emerged back out and vanished into another realm. Jnfr squatted down, and shivered: her huge frame appeared as if she was still standing. I saw the tension build in her legs, she was ready to spring…at me.

I leapt at her first to close the gap as quick as I could. The dress responded by closing its gap as well and forming into pants to give me better maneuverability.

I intended to bring down my full body weight on Jnfr's thigh with my feet. She avoided direct impact by shifting, which I anticipated for her to do. Instead, she took the brunt of the attack on her knee.

*Anyone else— even one of those wolves— would have had a broken leg!*

But, I knew that Jnfr would not be a fazed by it.

Somehow I knew her body as well as my own. She tumbled back and landed awkwardly on her side. Nevertheless, her foot came out to meet my chest, before I was able to mount her upper body. I turned to the side narrowly avoided the blow. Although her foot and shin scraped my chest and caused my suit to smoke from friction.

*What speed!*

*And I gather she'll be getting faster over time...must end this.*

I let my body slide in on her leg to get closer to her, then jammed my knee into her ribcage. She howled like an animal and bared her teeth. I paid no attention, just gladly accepted the flailing arm from the reaction of pain.

I straddled her arm and brought my other knee into her neck. The back of my head barely missed the side of the counter cabinet when I arched my hips forward. All her feral behavior subsided, once I struck her external lung point when the hyperextension of shoulder exposed it on her chest.

She passed out and I released her body. After untangling my body from hers, I stood up and checked myself for any wounds. Since, my body doesn't operate with its own separate consciousness anymore, I immediately felt the effects of the adrenaline rush when I began to fight.

There was no way to gauge how much force to use to avoid injury. It was like the first time feeling my body after such a long time.

Also, this planet operates on a very high density— much higher than my home-world or other planets I have visited.

Seeing that I was not harmed, I checked on Jnfr. Her hands clutched her chest, possibly involuntarily protecting herself just before passing out. Was she possessed?

*Or did she experience this thing called The Fever? I promised her mother I would watch over her and I intend to keep that promise.*

I lifted her body onto mine and lugged her downstairs to the pool. *Something in me says that this is the right thing to do.*

When I got her into the room, I noticed that everything was returned to its original pristine.

"Mu..." I called out to it.

It immediately sent out its watery arms towards us. Apparently the eye allowed me to be recognized by it, even command it. Mu took Jnfr off my back and gently brought her into the pool.

"Can you help her?" I called out from across the room. My voiced echoed throughout the open space and stillness of the room. Mu took humanoid form and glided back over. Its watery body paused in front of me before it lightly sprinkled me with water on my forehead.

The feeling was warm, inviting and communicated a gentle *"Yes,"* then it returned back to the pool. I left Mu to its task.

Once I got back upstairs, I was greeted by the aroma of the soup. It would be best to consume it before it ended up like the last batch. I poured myself a bowl, which was more like a bucket and sat below the large tekken hanging from the center of the ceiling.

I gave thanks for the food and brought the bowl to my

mouth. Everything in my mouth was filled with such wonderful tastes, all from simple ingredients. As far as I could tell, the soup was only composed of water, simple green vegetables and some nut-like granules.

Yet, they were energized to their highest vibrations regardless of being cooked. After reluctantly sipping the last of it, I sat my empty bowl aside and eased back, satiated as well as invigorated. I looked up and stared at the tekken; it started to flicker as the lights in the room dimmed.

For a moment, I thought I was in a theatre about to see a play or a moving picture as I have experienced on other worlds in various forms. Although, this was a basic living room, the height of its ceilings and spacious room still suggested otherwise.

Suddenly, an image of two figures in combat projected from its surface, both of them appeared prepared to send the other into the next world.

The crowd cheered in the stands above them: over them was the same type of misty red vapor streaming— fluctating with their excitement and screams. The opponents raged at one another seeking to draw more than blood.

Then, in an instant, one of them combusted into flames.

*Disgusting.*

For some reason, all these acts of violence offended me. I did not want to see this, nevertheless the images continued to bombard my senses. The weight of their bodies entered the room, the smell of musk spread through the room and dirt... sweat along with every other element became present.

Or at least my brain thought that it was taking place. These things once thrilled me, and now they only left a bitter taste on my tongue. I turned away from the projection, ashamed that something so trivial would have an effect on me.

The bitterness that filled my mouth painted a dull picture in my mind of my surroundings. I wanted that perception to leave. Seeking to rid myself of these feelings, thoughts of the caring attitude of my mother and Tzkw came through.

I was drawn to the window by the sunlight of the twin suns of this planet. Furniture and parts of the floor touched by their beams seem to emit excited particles from their surface. Rapidly dancing, moving in and out from their skins.

*I know from experience, that all things are part of a living mind.*

*And from this room, I can see those things*

*being an actual reflections of my own body.*

*I literally heard Jehuti's laughter in my head as he sat by his empty scroll tablets.*

What a jester! Reminds me of when we first settled Ta, our

home-world of solid matter long after our birth in air-pockets... when we gave each other titles.

*That fool always projected the akhu of an elder although I came into being before him.*

I turned my attention to the currents of sekhem as they flowed up to the ceiling. They raced across the baseline of the ceiling to the corners.

Suddenly, they spun rapidly then expanded before they contracted and vanished. All the walls burned with an incandescent white light, almost blinding. I shut my eyes still sensing the radiance.

Gradually the brightness that illuminated the inner walls of my eyelids faded, then something touched my face—nothing physical but filled with warmth. I opened my eyes and was met with a projection of individuals gathered at a table.

The tekken now pulsed blue along with an image of a family, eating and discussing their day.

Compassionate energies flooded the room along with the scents of their food and individual smells. All pleasant. All inviting. My mind began to feel at ease, I allowed the visions to further engage me.

*This must be a source of entertainment; tuning into events or shows that reflect a person's current mood.* I watched the family join their hands and give reverence for their food before they ate.

They worked in unison to share out the food, the elder of the family enjoyed receiving what look like the best part of the roasted beast. I could not tell if they were actors or an actual family.

The little ones watched their elders and mimicked their motions. And the elders took cues from their ancestors and surroundings. They fed one another food and expressed love in their actions. I so wanted to be there with them!

"Whenever you are ready, I am here." A voicc called out in my head. The image left just as abruptly as it came.

The ebb and flow of sunlight created by drifting clouds entered the room with a lulling effect on my senses. I sank deeper into the cushions, drawn in by their rustic comfort.

*What's next for me? My drive for conquest is running dry. My recollection of repressed memories and a sense of belonging all leaves me where?*

I heard something scratching at the door, starting off slow then turning into heavy pawing. Before I decided upon a course of action, Mu sprung out from the floor, splashing water everywhere. It raced to the door like a bright red flash, and then passed through its wood.

Sounds of tussling could be heard along with yelps and snapping of branches from the other side of the door. I reluctantly got up from my resting place and moved to the door.

I recognized the animal musk that virtually attacked my nerves. Another sharp cry filled my ears before I opened the door.

Mu had subdued the very same dog that brought me nourishment earlier on in the forest. It held him in a watery chokehold, while binding the rest of his body in its form. The dog gazed at me with a pitiful look for help.

"Mu let it *go.*" I commanded it.

Mu ignored me— red energy glowed brightly from its core, as it intensified the choke. The dog's tongue flew out its mouth and hung lazily. I noticed that Mu did not seem connected to the house any more. The path of water between it and the doorway had slowly receded.

A primal sensation tugged at our link, Mu was taking on the nature of the wild— it meant to kill him. I cautiously approached Mu, so not to set it off, and placed my hands on its surface.

I needed to open my heart to reconnect it back to it to house…but I didn't know how. I felt emotionally blocked and clumsy, my heart swelled with emotions of my son.

And then, when I saw the dog's eyes pleading with me for his life. In that moment, I was able to connect. I opened up. As I fed it my presence, Mu calmed itself and released the dog.

It embraced me and although its body was cool to the touch, it was warm. Mu retreated back into the house, leaving me with a frightened large dog panting and shaking on the ground.

"You risked a lot by coming here! What is it you want?"

"I came to warn you about the serpent who seeks you out!" He blurted out in between pants.

"Serpent? After me?" I only knew of one serpent that would…it *couldn't* be him.

"Our new ruler has sent my brothers out to capture you. He is a large serpent that carries a strange man-spirit."

*It is him.*

*My husband.*

"We met before. What do they call you?" I asked.

"I am called Wp." He whimpered.

My asking of his name allowed him to relax a bit, although he stayed on guard.

Wp suddenly picked his head up and looked towards the thick bush and trees that surrounded the house.

*Sniff. Sniff. More of that terrible smell is on the air; not difficult to distinguish it from others. More of his kind are on the way.*

Wp cringed, backing up into my side almost knocking me down. *He must think they'll deal with him harshly for being here.*

I stroked his head to his neck then shoulders, my fingers got tangled every so often in his thick mane along the way. I scratched in between the blades, he beat his tail wildly against the ground, scattering leaves and grass.

"It is alright young one. We will figure something out," I spoke softly to him.

Although his pack was getting close, his anxiety began to wane. He turned his head to me and looked submissively into my eyes. "When I am of age, you may have my flesh if you wish." He spoke with honorable intent.

"Little one, I am touched by your sentiment. But I do not eat flesh of other beings as a choice." He seemed dismayed by my words. "However, if the need ever rises, I can think of no other I wish to combine with to accomplish my goal."

Wp licked my face from his standing position, I could see he wanted to jump on me, but knew he would knock me down. I am literally like a child on this world.

To see the cycles and reciprocity of life play out in interaction between beings without it forced upon them, is enlightening to my being.

Slowly the atmosphere drew in on itself and became thick with hostility and an undercurrent tone of reluctance.

*Were they coming against their own wills? In his will?*

Along with the general atmosphere, the spiritual pressure became denser and denser. The soles of my bare feet picked up on the increasing tremors that were rippling through the earth.

Soon the entire area shook as their deathly howls were heard in the distance. All plant-life curled their stems in, exposing their hard sides for protection. All the grass around us pulled into the earth, setting off what looked like a wave, leaving only the tips to be seen from out the ground. They excreted a light mist into the air that immediately irritated my exposed skin.

In response, the material in the neck and cuffs of my battle-suit, excreted a mist of its own which counteracted the effects. It appeared to have taken its cue from my wrap-skirt, I could feel electric current flowing between the two, each with its own signature.

My feet were not effected, thanks to eons of conditioning on the battle-field they developed enough callous around them to protect my pores.

On the other hand, Wp quickly rustled his fur, creating enough friction to vaporize the mist when it came too close to him.

Something caused me to look up at the branches of the tree near me. It swayed back and forth, rustling its leaves then released a chemical in my direction. I was able to see the fields around the chemical before it came in contact with my nose. This was the communication that happened earlier when the surroundings would speak to me on the air, yet, now I am able to actually perceive it.

Once I took its aroma in, I was able to identify it in the folds of my memory. This happened before— only thing I wasn't aware of it. Trees usually used this communication to protect others from harm, and help each other to grow, an age-old survival mechanism.

*They must feel that they must help me in order to preserve the life cycles of their brethren.*

It spoke. "*You are partially correct. We look to preserve all life that have not yet reached the ending of their cycles, along with preserving our own.*" It answered in response to my pondering. "*Find the one who is the mightiest amongst them and make him yours.*"

As before the words came with the wind but, they came clearer and with ease of intention. I knew exactly what I could do to identify the strongest of their pack.

But first, I had to deal with Wp. His flesh would not be

spoiled— especially since it was promised to me.

I brought Wp to lie down and crouched down besides him. I scratched behind his ears, he turned his head side to side, beating his tail hard against the ground. Gradually I rolled my fingers to his neck then squeezed with enough force for him to pass out.

After I seen that Wp was completely unconscious, I dragged him back to the house where Mu stood in the doorway. "Protect him. Protect Jnfr and the house." It nodded.

Before I left, Mu handed me some type of dried bark and motioned for me to chew it. I took it from its hand and hesistantly placed it in my mouth. As I chewed on it, the door closed and then a wave of water gently crashed over the house, becoming misty then invisible.

Some type of natural cloaking mechanism. The bark was sweet and almost a pleasure to chew on. When the juices went down my throat, I felt something strange. Instead of it entering my stomach, it somehow entered my bloodstream and traveled within them to my feet.

Once there, it left the bloodstream and headed for my flesh, then excreted out my pores. They engulfed my feet from sole to ankle with a material that felt like leather footwear.

I had a distinctive memory of how Jnfr's footwear

looked when she first found me. I keyed into that memory and fed it to my new footwear. They took on the same shape along with a layer of rubbery traction on the soles.

I moved away from the house and got on all fours. Through my palms and toes, I drove my Ka into the ground, attaching it to roots and rocks.

In an instant, the direction of the pack was revealed by the rocks and roots that reeled intensely from the tremors. Along with the grass that released more of its mist than other areas. They were coming up from the north— masking their scents as they rushed towards us.

*No matter, unlike before, I am able to sense their physical bodies...regardless of where they hide.*

I drew in my breath, pulling in the sekhem around me, taking whatever I wished from the house as well. As my lungs filled, I arched my back up and pulled in force from the ground; collapsing the earth underneath me.

The trees seeing to the heart of what I planned to do, gave more sekhem of what they allowed me to collect. Once my lungs were full, I dropped my abdomen and pushed out everything I took in.

"RAAAAAA!" The sound flew wildly out my mouth, shaking my teeth and lips as it left.

The heavy field of the wave blanketed everything in the northernly direction with concussive force laying flat just about everything in its path. Only those that could withstand the onslaught were able to re-absorb the energy without mishap.

Once the blast reached the pack the same effect took place, only leaving one of them able to bare the brunt of the impact. His stance remained strong for the duration yet he was not able to take it in. That resistance reverberated back to me.

The wave that struck back at me not only carried his contempt for me but also his form, hear-rate and even scent—all imprinted on the wind. From my lowered position, I dug my feet into the earth and burst into speed, heading for the area that they occupied.

As I ran, I sent forth a lesser blast to incapacitate any one of them coming to their wits. Within breaths I reached them and seized the dog by the neck. He thrashed about until I applied pressure to the ditch between his jaw and ear. The pain made him quickly go from gnashing at me to gritting his teeth.

"Calm down or I will send another blast into your ears, leaving your pack without a hope against your usurper." I whispered into his ear with a subtle burst that reflected my threat.

He eased his tension and I released his neck. "How can

you— a mere pet— be of any use to us?" he asked, taking care not to anger me.

"I know things of him that you do not. Leave it at that." I placed a small link onto his brain stem. He let out a small yelp.

*It is good to see that my abilities are returning to me or should I say I am now free to use them. My synergy with the All Nature seems to be improving.*

As my thought finished, I felt a slight pinch in the link. I let Np, the name carried by his consciousness, know that I meant him and his pack no harm.

That I was only after Apep.

When his brethren recovered, they all turned their attention to me and bared their teeth. Np let out a resounding bark that caused his brethren to shriek in fear.

"You will not harm her! She will come willingly with us!"

Much of his kindred were still skeptical, as expected, they began to growl and snap their teeth.

"Knock me out and take me to Pp." I sent secretly to Np along the link.

I did not have to warn him about betrayal because his Akhu carried no such intent. He was a proud and honorable warrior of his pack. Although the heavy paw that pummeled my face could of easily took my head off...

Sleep was coming soon. Things around me grew dark as he took my neck into his mouth...

N

## *Chapter Medju Sesu*
## *Duat*

After my eyelids sluggishly rose fully open, the sight of Apep looming over me rushed blood and sekhem into my eyes.

The rough patch of earth underneath me, scraped and stung at my back as I scampered back in surprise—keeping my attention on his huge horrid scaly body.

The bulk of it blocked most of the beautiful mid-day sky from my sight. I wanted to laugh outloud at the fact that I could notice beauty at a time like this. Then in mid-thought, my breath ran shallow and light-headedness beat against my focus.

Next came the awareness of saturated depressive Ka seeking to wrap around the welling up of my emotions, disturbing my otherwise stoic demeanor. Spirits of the plant-life screamed out in pain, reflecting their charred surfaces—offering only tainted air to breathe.

Tree after tree lay twisted on the ground, most of them snapped at the bark and smoldering. The stagnation and humidity of the atmosphere drained into the passing of patches of thick misty fog.

*I am no stranger to a sight like this yet, it does not offer the same welcome as it did before.*

Apep sensing the subtle change in my heart, lowered his head to me, he let loose his jaw and lightly raked his fang across my cheek.

When my blood trickled out, his tail vigorously thrashed about scattering dirt and sediment. I pushed aside his head and raised myself up onto my elbows.

He abruptly stopped to glare into my eyes as if to say, *I have you now.*

"I have you now." The words finally left his mouth. After all his juvenile behavior.

My lips pulled tight together, unable to relax to express anything. However, the tears came easy. Burying my head in between my legs, I longed for a sword to cut at the pain. I cried for the all the memories that came pouring forth and for every moment that lead to this confrontation.

Apep —the only name I can remember him by— reveled

in the excitement of finally catching me. The mood in his camp became increasingly ominous, an uneasy tension flowed in the link between Np and myself.

*"What is your strategy?"* Np sent to me. *"My people…want to see action. Or they will more than happily tear out your throat…pet."* Np concluded and was sure to include the resolve of his Ka: it was no threat.

His pack considered themselves trapped in a forced obligation with someone who did not honor any of their tribal ways.

"Do you ever think about our son?" Apep asked unexpectedly, he'd ceased his movement after he coiled around me.

I wanted to answer no, because until yesterday he was nonexistant to me. But without my telling him directly, he seemed to know already. His facial expression grew grim.

Yet, when his eyes met mine, only a glint of humanity was visible in them...the rest Esfet.

"I *see."* He constricted his body around me until I could only breathe. Nothing more.

His tongue lashed out at my face, the wetness of it slapped heavy into my cheekbones. I stood still as it flicked about my face; coating it with thick pats of saliva that hung before it dropped. My skin went numb from traces of venom in it.

"You have grown. Your taste tells me your little identity problem is resolved." He lessened the pressure of his grip.

Apep uncoiled from my upper body, but kept me bound from the waist down to keep me from falling over. My arms hung limply at my sides, he stroked them with his tongue lightly paralyzing them with toxins. They were already weakened by his gentle crush, so I knew this was his way of showing his dominance.

"Yet, you have forgotten our son…the one you drove against me. The one who murdered me." His voice grew sullen.

"It was only at the final instant when his blade met my skull, did I remember our seed." Apep dragged on.

"Have you had enough of my tears?" I cut through his attempt to torture me with words. "Do they resolve or speak to anything in your heart?" I asked plainly.

"Your tears do appease me but they speak nothing to what I do not have!" he retorted.

*I want to help him, yet there is no room to plead with someone who has lived for eternity.*

"Well, do what you have wanted to for so long!" I chose to go through this without my fists. "I will not fight you." I sat on my insteps and lifelessly dropped my hands to the damp ground.

"Yes...it is time." Apep's tongue slapped the sides of his face.

He rose up over me and flung his jaw open wide. The heat and stench from his breath came down heavy on me... just before his mouth.

He swallowed me whole.

*This is what he'd wanted for so long—to make me a part of him without any separation...*

*It is dark and cold within his body like the vastness of space...*

His walls drove me deep into him. Immediately my suit and dress spread over all the exposed areas of my body. Once my face was covered, the suit's skin around my eyes slowly became transparent allowing me to see.

I did not stop to think that the inside of Apep would be volatile to me. Yet the dissolving sound of my suit said otherwise.

Without my permission, sekhem was sucked from out my pores to reconstitute its skin. After a few attempts, it was able to create a shell strong enough to hold together without further repair.

Meanwhile my dress worked equally hard to absorb whatever acid that came in contact with it. By way of our rapport, I saw it transformed the acid into oxygen and readily digestible sugars.

Although the restructure of molecules at that level seemed beyond laws of alchemy for a symbiote, I didn't refuse it being fed into me. Once the fresh oxygen and base nourishment ran its course, I was able to regain my poise, still shaken with all the coming and going of processes.

Ever since the transference of the eye, subtle shifts of sekhem between myself and this planet have taken place. The strength of the atmospheric pressure has lightened, and the air more receptive of my intake.

Apparently those shifts have allowed me to access my own natural abilities, that were shunted off from me with my arrival.

Another thing was clear. This planet —who was the sister of my beloved Ta— was in a sense my *aunt.*

And Khusat, my aunt's utterance of Akhu, was not as hostile towards me as before.

Khusat had shown me things, things that allowed me to formulate a plan while I'd riden in slumber on Np's back to Apep.

I opened a small portal into the void of Khusat and sent a pulse from my eye to contact Mu.

On the other side, Mu was startled by the small portal that

opened into its domain, nevertheless it immediately recognized my essence flowing out of it. I requested the same mix of substances that took me through my transition... except in a stronger dose. Mu assembled the concoction in seconds and forwarded it through the portal.

I rubbed my temples, and closed the portal upon receipt of the pack. Then I fixed my mind on the location to arrive at after stepping whole body into the void of Khusat.

And not a second too soon!

*Apep's digestive system found a way around my suit's defense... its acids have begun to eat fervently into its layers and then my skin.*

I lodged the pack into one of its ducts and opened a door into the void. I stepped into it— barely saving my arm from complete corrosion— leaving Apep's insides responding violently to the powder.

"Don't *go...!*" Apep's consciousness whispered, his voice rasped in depletion.

I shut the door quickly to avoid any of its tissues being pulled in behind me. Once in the void, it took time for my eyes to adjust to the brightness of its vast neural net of souls that connected everything and everyone.

From a distance I was able to see Jnfr suffering the torment of fighting off The Fever. Mu kept her suspended in its waters, painstakingly sweeping her cells of all traces of it.

Following the locked position of the place I could arrive at, I opened the door. These trips required the use of my merkaba and an exchange of some sort of energy; which meant *something* had to stay behind. I left the acid that trailed me into the void along with pieces of my burned flesh.

Once through, I quickly took refuge in the highest tree I could find, although with only one usable arm. Then I contacted Np: "Pp will fall into a deep slumber as soon as the suns vanish from sight."

*"Is there anything we need to be concerned about?"* he sent back.

"Yes. He will attempt to take as many of your men as possible. Withdraw *now.* He will be shedding his skin in an unusual manner."

Np acknowledged the severity of the situation, glanced briefly towards my direction. I embraced the branch and remained still.

An impression of familiarity came over me. Apep writhed in agony, attempting to fight off the cleansing of his being. He lashed out at whoever was around him, sinking his fangs into those who were not fast enough to evade him. Those that he did catch were desperately sucked at their necks.

Maybe he thought their blood would dilute what was

placed inside of him. Finding that his blood rampage did nothing to better his condition, he retreated to his hole. His rough scaly hide ripped from off him as he side-winded across the ground.

After a while, the painful scrapes across his naked un-molted hide left Apep at a slow crawl. Finally he made it to his hole and plunged into it. Most of his battered and bruised pulpy body made it in except for his tail. It whipped about protruding out the entrance.

Some of Np's pack howled in glee and took swipes at it until the whole ordeal became one bloody mess. Np growled loudly then turned his head from the clamor and headed out the camp. Wildly animated from the end of their subservient role, his brethren pulled in their spirits until they were calm once more and followed behind him.

He glimpsed up at me, then away. A sharp pinch tugged at the back my neck. Apep snapped the link. Something he could have done at anytime.

Once there was no trace of their scent in the air, I came down the tree. My steps were staggered by the weight of my heart, the gentle breeze and the approach of the night.

An intoxicating spirit of pain and fatigue filled my being, the rush of it only further confused my soul. I made my way over to the entrance, along the way my mouth grew dry and my eyelids stung...wanting to close... wanting sleep

Grief filled my lungs making them constrict and dense with wetness. Breathing became labored, I collapsed to the ground hitting my knees.

The vacant limb of Apep, my husband, lay in front of me: ripped to shreds. Pieces were scattered amongst the burnt plants. My body coursed with sekhem and was fully revitalized. Yet, none of that mattered. I could not move.

The anger that filled his being was stripped away from him, the drive for chaos had finally met the end of its cycle. Just as both suns have left the sight of this arena...

* * *

I must have passed out because I cannot account for lost time. Even with the night sky providing its luminence, a pitch black veil blanketed the area. Slowly other spectrums of light opened up to my vision.

With the absence of solar energy to keep the esfet in check, all repressed emotional and natural nocturnal forces roamed freely. Spirits similar to the ones encountered back at the house, came and went, without the slightest interest in me.

My nose stung from the musky odor that filled the air, and told me there were many visitors as I slept. Apparently they picked over me leaving only superficial scratches.

*Maybe they prefer to devour something that is already wounded.* At least that's what crossed my mind before I saw a group of creatures by Apep's tail.

They were tearing into the hole, looking to get at what remained of him.

"*Noooo!*" I could not hold myself back any longer. My scream managed to turn their attention away from Apep and towards me. One's slobbering jaws pointed in my direction and I wasn't going to give him the chance to rush.

Before it could dig its paws into the ground to leap, I lunged at it first. My two fingers pierced deep into its eye until they contacted muscles and nerves. It screamed out as I clenched chord and tissue, then rolled finger over finger until it was tightly entwined.

With a sharp and unflinching wrench, its eye and all that was attached to it was relieved from its socket. His life fluids gushed out violently and splashed my suit then slid off.

He clutched for my arms, desperately trying to get a grip on me. Meanwhile, the other creatures—heightened by the threat that their meal might be taken away—dug frantically into the hole.

I managed to get on top of the wailing creature's head. I stood on it for a moment, steadied my balance, then jumped. When I landed I increased my density by three-fold, which took a toll on my entire body... as all my molecules shifted from one state to another rapidly.

It tried to resist by stiffening the muscles in its huge neck. But it snapped.

I rode its face into the ground and leapt off, leaving its limbs twitching. My heart raced, not out of personal fear, but out of fear for my husband's torment.

Then I heard his muddled cries from beyond the hole, urging me on to my next foe. I cracked the long chord of tendon and nerve like a whip at the last two beasts. They took the strikes head-on without flinching, it did not deter them from the need to feed.

I increased the speed of the recoils, almost approaching supersonic speeds on the drawbacks. Had not my body's cell structure withstood the opposing force of pressure, my arm and all the bones inside me would have exploded.

But I tore at my shoulder all the same. The fibers of my tendons expanded pass their threshold and nearly left my good arm useless.

*No matter, I must see my husband!*

I lunged at the beasts cringing in pain and clawed at the air. Their long tongues licked at the deep lacerations that burnt through their thick coats.

They came at me fast, the first one I took easily moving pass its thrashing arms and razor pinchers. The blood drenched cord ,which still lay in my grip, was now wrapped around its neck. I swung my body around to its back using the tauntness of the chord.

I got myself in a good position, avoiding the protruding spike-like protrusions littered across its skin and began to strangle it. It coughed and gagged..and fought just as hard to remain conscious.

Not one of its many arms could reach me—so moving about ferociously, to shake me off, was its next move. The strength needed to properly strangle it escaped me, my burned arm and strained shoulder could not keep the posture necessary for pressure.

"My love they will *not* have you!" I spoke aloud to the night air.

I decided to go against all the warning signs of my body and intensified all my muscles, sekhem flooded all fibers like a surging stream. My exposed bone finally dislodged from my elbow, though I did not scream out. As the surrounding esfet filled-air poured into the opening, I grew weak. My dress responded with lightning quick reflexes, scooped up a bit of cool earth from out the ground, re-attached my elbow and bonded it like a makeshift cast.

The cool dressing relieved my anxiety although I began to wonder why it waited so long to take this action. I knew that the cast would only hold long enough for me to finish my task.

Another creature stalked around us looking for an opening. I drew in a deep breath and screamed into the beast's ear. Its brains tore out the top of its skull and onto its partner's face.

I pushed off the corpse, and twisted my body in the air to land on the final adversary who was still in the middle of clearing its face of pulverized brain. Without a second thought, I pounded his sternum until I heard something crack... and kept on after that sound met both of our ears.

It swung at my face, and each time it did I merely evaded the strike and pounded harder. I forgot myself, my skill and no longer knew why I was hitting it. Hard bone gave way to soft tissue, soft tissue to organs.

I abruptly came to a halt and looked down at the mess I created. My lungs felt like they were going to burst. The beast's akhu was literally beat out of its body. I know this because I sensed traces of its fleeing sekhem all about its hulking mass.

In the midst of all that took place—along with my bruised hands painted with its insides—purity overwhelmed my being.

*I fought to protect a loved one for an opportunity to settle two hearts.*

Drained, I climbed off its body while attempting to rub off the parts of caked blood that would fleck off my hands. Not caring to look down, the sense of purity rapidly changed to indifference.

*The hole—!*

I kneeled down and pulled at whatever obstructed the entrance, plunging my arm into the cavity of Apep, tearing through hardened tissue and guts. I projected my Ka down within to scan ahead before entering.

It tunneled through, unable to expand further than a little over the circumference of my own body. After a while, it finally widened out to an open space. I drew it back. My Ka disseminated the impressions that were made upon it.

Then I realized, Apep had shed more than his skin. He'd shed his entire serpent shell.

Overwhelmed with the prospect of what state I may find him in, I thrusted my other arm in and pulled myself into him. Climbing through became challenging... as the remaining awareness of his cells drew upon the sekhem in its walls to obstruct my path.

My suit and dress once again shielded me and began fending off the natural defenses. I projected my Ka once more all about me, to operate like a second set of eyes. The lack of light from its bodily functions and amassed esfet made it as dark.

As I made my way through the mucous and fat, that latched onto to me excreting whatever toxins still left in its bowels, I found myself unattached.

The more this atmosphere imposed its will on me to prevent me from reaching my husband, the more I let go of frustration and anxiety.

*Whatever will be, will be.*

After pulling apart a wall of tightly wound guts, a crushed and mangled body of one of Np's brethren became visible. It lay wedged in the intestines: flattened and drained of all fluids except for the ones that came from Apep swaddling its form.

I drove forward, knowing that I neared the mouth. No other contact was made with any of the other organs. It was as if they'd been removed.

Finally, I emerged out from the last bit of the dog's shed decomposing flesh.

Khat, the name I decided to give to the unison of my suit

and dress, drew from the ample moisture in the air and caused it to shower upon me—washing away all decay and toxic fluids. Next it raised its temperature and released it through its pores to dry me off.

*Did the Khemenu Nebu have some higher reason for hurtling me on this planet and equipping me with such a symbiote?*

I advanced cautiously into an ominous cold dank tunnel, my resolve grew despite the smells that forbade me to move further. Following my extended Ka, I avoided creatures that lay in wait...along with the poisonous roots that moved toward me with my every step.

Upon entering a clearing there was a sudden drop in temperature—much colder, much darker than the rest of the chambers.

The outline of Apep's body became apparent to me, along with his indistinguishable scent…his *returned* scent. The thought of engaging the sekhem in my eyes to perceive more than just shadows came and went. It was better to be in the darkness with him.

He lay in a crude plot in the soft earth. The first thing that was noticeable, even in this murkiness, was nails filled with dirt, some hanging off the fingers.

*Apparently he frantically scraped and clawed at dirt to make his bed for transition.*

His weakened body was covered in left-over traces of membranes and fluid from his old form. Slowly I knelt down beside him then laid on top of him, not minding that his skin literally suctioned against my own.

It was still hardening. I did not care to look at him face to face. It was enough just to hold and feel him.

"My love…my memories are still coming back…most of them," I whispered into his ear, my lips peeled back moist tissue from his lobe.

His body trembled with each word that he heard, as if the sound alone caused him pain.

I ran my hands over him, doing my best not to pull back when they touched misshapened bone and missing flesh.

"Neith...Ankh E...Mer E..." he rasped out names that triggered old memories of how we once were.

He attempted to move us both from out the plot, but collapsed back into it from lack of strength. Pulling me down with him I collapsed onto him, he almost bucked me off in response to pian.

"I was strong once, wasn't I?" His voice no longer sounded like a serpent...and yet not quite like a man.

"Rest my love. What is done is done." I stroked his naked

scalp talking care not pull out any of the loosely rooted scattered tuffs of hair.

"*Wasn't* I?" The question came again along with his hand barely able to remove mine from his head.

"Yes... As strong as a thousand Medjay."

"Thank you." He paused then coughed up some bile. "Hearing those words from you makes it easier to forget."

He drifted...then passed out.

"Forget what. What is there to forget?" I shook him back to consciousness, holding his arms so tight that it bruised his flaccid skin.

"Forget that I welcomed Apep. That I allowed my blood thirst during the war with the Serpents to overtake me," he answered, his voice could barely be heard.

*He will not have long before he enters the Duat.*

"That you forced our unborn son out your womb to hunt me...Women's scorn." He laughed then coughed and shook fiercely.

When the last of his strained words left his mouth, they immediately triggered a sharp migraine—a repressed memory that pushed out from the center of my brain and burned into my thoughts. Series of images flashed before my eyes without rhythm and sequence.

"Are you doing this? Stop now!" I pleaded with him to no avail.

All this was too much to digest in such a small space of time.

*Too much pain, too much hurt.*

My stomach cramped and burned, I hobbled away from him to a corner and spat up whatever was held in it. Returning back to him, I increased the amount of saliva in my mouth, whished it around then spat out the horrible taste.

Uncontrollable flashes of memories beat around in my head, with enough intensity to claw out from my skull. Regardless of the stress that I am sure damaged tissue. I was able to quiet the pulsation of rapidly playing events and arrange them in a comprehendible sequence.

*Khnum was right. When Khnum allowed the tide of war to overtake him, he was no longer a Netcher of a man, he became Apep.*

In my frustration and anger, our son's akhu and Ka was forced prematurely out my belly.

Once its essence hit the external world, the surrounding earth and my hatred drew in to fashion its physical body. His empty husk of physical material within me reabsorbed itself into my cells.

We hunted Khnum for centuries, finally we caught up with

him and my son, Sa Sekhmet, slayed him…at least that's what we thought.

Somehow, he came back from whatever pit he was cast into and took Sa Sekhmet—he took him and devoured him.

After that time, I roamed aimlessly through the world and then the cosmos. My impaired mind sought war and vengeance on anyone or anything. Memories of my son were buried deeper and deeper with every swing of my sword.

Numerous times the Duat took me into her arms, and each time I escaped judgement—becoming stronger and faster and more imbalanced.

Yet the dormant cells of my son didn't stay quiet for long. Soon they re-awakened and slowly imparted their being into what was...

To become Khat.

Still gathering myself, I leaned over Khnum and looked at him longingly. All around his body, cold energy blanketed him.

"Khnum...?" he was gone.

I sat there crying until my eyes shut from strained use. Was it all over? Nothing was resolved. What I knew about the every lasting circle of life conflicted with the way Khnum's cold and departed shell lay in front of me.

*What purpose am I left with?* Not a thought or answer came

to console me. Only darkness.

A soft glow gradually illuminated the lair, its radiance grew brighter and brighter. In my despair, I failed to recognize it was coming from me.

The left side of my body released an orange light while the right shone a gold brilliance. In a matter of moments, the Ka of two animal spirits crept from out my arms respectively and sat themselves by Khnum's corpse.

One was Wadjet, the other Sekhmet.

"We are here to bring into existence that which still beckons for a form." They spoke in unison.

Wadjet rose up and dove into Khnum and Sekhmet pounced into me.

Khnum sprung up and took me into his arms. He pressed his chest against mine, its renewed warmth aroused everything within me. I squeezed him with all my strength. This time his body could take it.

My suit, Khat, sensing it was not needed at the present moment, slipped off my body and formed itself into a small mat. Khnum wasted no time in bringing us both onto it.

Our bodies continued to radiant, filling the entire chamber with charged light. All creatures that were quietly lurking about scurried away from the pulses of energy. Their claws and paws could be heard scrambling across the ground.

Khnum kissed me deeply and passionately while caressing my hips. His manhood throbbed against my thigh, building in strength and heat. The anticipation and suddenness of the situation caused.

My womb grew hot and my heart fluttered in my chest. It began to draw upon the elements of my entire essence. Besides nutrients and blood, it sifted through my memories and extracted detailed information.

It also took from the dormant consciousness of the former Khat.

It was forming an egg.

Khnum's virility poured out from his skin, causing my arousal to heighten.

"I am going to leave you with a part of me."

His strong fingers gently crawled in between my legs, I could not help but to shiver. Khnum parted my legs and entered in between my lips. They kissed my husband's manhood with no recollection of when they'd last enjoyed its presence.

At first his firm strokes were a bit unpleasant due to my inactivity but then my womb yielded to his insistence and opened its walls...

I held him by the waist as he drove deeper and faster. At

this moment if I were to suddenly lose all awareness of myself for all time to come, I would not care.

Every part of me was stirred up with an intense fire that imbued all my cells. Our eyes met and became one, then within that meeting we became unaware of each other. We were whole.

We moved together, giving and taking of one another until our sweat became sweet.

"Take care…of me."

Before I could pull myself from ectasy to respond, his life-germ flooded my walls. The warm sensation of his fluid spread throughout my womb and raced up my spine bringing about my own climax. Just then, a cool rush of air filled the chamber.

My glance in the direction of it noticed the protruding roots from the walls nervously swaying in the breeze.

Suddenly Khnum began to shake and tremble, a cracking sound like bones snapping came from his chest. His whole upper body caved-in and pulled into his lower abdomen.

Rather than averting my eyes, I watched: this was the same process that Sa Sekhmet can to be born—except in reverse.

It was necessary.

He smiled with not the least bit of anxiety or complaint on his face. Without wavering, my love remained stalwart during the echoing of his entire mass folding in.

"My *love...!"* I called out faintly to him.

After awhile, all that was left of him was a brilliant mass of sekhem surrounding his Akhu. Then in a quick burst all of his energies were swept into a vacuum that drew into my womb. Within me, the newly formed egg took in every part of Khnum and blossomed with light like the rays of Ra.

I was now with child.

Shock and awareness grappled with my reasoning as I sat on Khat drenched in our unified sweat and covered with his scent.

Alone.

But, that was short-lived once another wave of cold air eeiringly breezed through the lair, carrying with it a most foul intent.

Khat immediately reacted by embracing my body and fortifying its layers. Although it sensed the heightened sekhem within me, it fed me nourishment from its stores. Khat sensed the new life within me.

Until now, I did not notice that it also incorporated the secreted footwear into its being as well. sekhem flowed briskly to my eyes, almost involuntarily, strengthening the structure of their operation and allowing me to see other things.

Beyond stimulating my natural compacity to see a large amount of spectrum of light, it enhanced the ability to perceive things that wished to keep themselves hidden.

Esfet marshaled the energy of all that it infested, and pulled it towards the lifeless serpent shell at the entrance. Something squirmed around my feet then quickly sped off, rodents and insects as huge as small dogs rushed towards the hole.

They collectively headed in the direction of the stream of murky mist that was gathered from the esfet in the tunnels and lair.

I followed without hesistance, sensing something menacing and familiar at the same time. Any other time these creatures may have either attacked or avoided me. Despite that, they seem to have ignored my close proximity to them as they rushed onward.

They appeared to be mesmerized by whatever was beyond this cavern. A forbading feeling shot throughout my spine and my vessels swelled with adrenalin. My nose became highly irritated, and my fists tightly wound. Stealth which would be the best choice to continue into the tunnel was overridden with the heart pounding skhm of ma'at. And it was ma'at that pushed me into the clearing.

# N

The esfet *did* have a destination. It fed the bodies of four pale, almost translucent-skinned ,beings. All of whom stopped their feeding of Apep's decaying flesh clumped in their hands and looked hungrily at me.

*I have met their kind before.*

*The Alde.*

# N

## *Chapter Medju Sefheku*
## *The Fold*

*What will I do now? Cower here in the folds of the All Nature?*

*No. Running—more like floating here—is not the answer. That will only prolong the inevitable rematch between Drrn and myself.*

"Drnn I, Kvn, will push you out your troubled shell the next time we meet!" I yelled out into the empty space.

My voice echoed out in front me without meeting anything to obstruct it. Ever since I arrived here, moist web-like projections sprung out at me and latched onto my exposed skin.

Others somehow ate through my clothing, the ripping sound they made into the fibers sounded like chewing. And they continued, until they contacted my skin and began to suck at it.

From every direction they came— with so much speed and number that if I let them they would swallow me. As I ripped the webs away, their reluctant suctions dragged themselves along my flesh and secreted chemicals that burned.

Suddenly they eased up their merciless attack and left me be. And not a moment too soon, I was nearly drained of all my physical shkm.

As much as I wanted to move, all I could do was let myself drift in space and watch the smoke from chemical burns, float off. In the distance, there were other visitors so engulfed only their limbs could be seen sticking out of globes of tangled webs.

Their bloodcurdling screams of anguish stabbed at my eardrums, only slightly muffled by the weightlessness of this place. Desperately they clawed at the webs and cried out until their voices went hoarse; their echoes rolled out in the empty space... then silence prevailed.

The sight of them struggling for their life only to end up as what appeared to me to be food, brought me no comfort.

*Is this the true reality of the All Nature? Are we just food once its true face is revealed?*

Since my father was held captive during the period when training was usually taught, I never learned how to use Hn or mentally defend myself.

*And the slow healing wounds Drrn left me with, don't make it any easier.*

*"Quiet yourself."* A voice spoke in my head. *"Stop rambling on. You are wasting your strength with thoughts that will solve nothing."* It came again.

"Who and what are you?" I questioned the voice outloud.

*"Have you forgotten me already?"*

The voice was not familiar to me at all. Or maybe I was too anxious to be able to recognize it.

*"I am your father,"* it called out to me.

"Why can't I see you?" I looked from side to side in vain.

*"What difference would that make now,"* he spoke sternly. *"Seeing me will not stop you attacking yourself?"*

"Attacking *myself?"* I asked, more confused than when he first started to talk.

*"Yes. Your fear drives the folds of The All Nature to defense. The fear makes them more inquisitive. They want to know what causes it."* Father kept on describing things that I had little grasp of.

"So you're saying not to do a thing when they approach me?" I almost pleaded with him.

*"Well, you see what violence and struggle has gotten you, and the others that stepped into the folds. Do nothing and nothing will happen."*

His advice wasn't very good. Nothing was practical about

standing still, while being swarmed by something I knew nothing about.

*"That's all,"* he added and ceased all further communication.

The space around me came to a standstill. I reached out for him in my thoughts, but he didn't respond. As nervous and frightened as I was, I didn't call out for him anymore. There was no point.

Looking for the same comfort that everyone on this world was able to receive in their link with The All Nature, I attempted to compose myself. But the air became thick with waves of cold pressure—like it was taking all friendship and warmth from me.

Then the webs sprung out from the surrounding walls once more. But this time, thinking about what my father said, I allowed them to contact me... their tips prodded about my body before they clung onto my skin.

Everything about them, had me wanting to lash out. Nonetheless I kept still.

Sharp electrical impulses pinched at my skin. With each small jolt something more than thoughts was being drawn out of me. After awhile they released me, possibly disinterested or having already figured out my intentions. I didn't care as long as they let me be.

They snapped their attention from me and raced over to someone else—someone who struggled to rip them off his body. Despite the weightlessness and him being a distance from me, a light scent of burned flesh quickly reached my nose.

He valiantly struggled against them...until his revolt forced more of them out…en masse. Disattaching themselves from the neural walls, they swarmed him— someone my age who, like myself, did not possess the ability to defend himself.

He was built like an ox, but that mattered for nothing. They overtook him easily and sucked him dry. Covered in them, his arm broke free and clutched at air... they wrapped around it like a serpent and yanked it back in.

Soon the ball of throbbing nerves contracted... until all that was left was a perfect sphere of light about the size of my fist. Once everything settled and it was no longer pulsing, it simply floated back to the wall and was slowly dissolved into it.

The walls seemed miles away from where I was suspended weightlessly in space. Although the gaps in between them glowed in different spectrums of light, the most dominate was violet.

The anxiety that arrested me earlier was gone. I found myself able to move about freely...just by setting my mind to it.

# N

“Do you know how to leave here?”A voice from behind startled me. There was no sound of movement before it. No way of telling there was someone near.

Once thing for sure. It wasn’t father.

I whipped my neck around and what my peripheral caught first, caused my heart to race with surprise.

A nude boy...like I'd never seen before. A male— but not exactly like myself. He was slim and tall, yet athletic with stringy hair and pale skin without color.

When he raised his arm to hail me, I practically saw his blood vessels and nerves. He drew closer to me and the way he carried his body did not reflect his stature.

He was not the child that he appeared to be.

“You look like you may know.” He placed a hand on my arm.

Ice. His touch was beyond cold and his voice carried a bit of emptiness in it. It was... distant. I eased back from him allowing his hand to slip off me naturally.

“Uh—yeah.” I decided to be casual about the whole situation. Although something told me to trounce his ass as soon as I had a chance.

“I can get out any time I wish.” I said confidently.

“Apparently this is your first time.” I finished.

I laid a hand back on his shoulder then briskly took it off shaking off the coldness of it.

"You look to be from the Nothern Nkh mountains. What tribe do you hail from?" This was all bullshit, no such mountain existed. I just wanted to see his response.

"The upper-most tip of course." He smiled.

He was lying…and he knew that I knew it. The muscles in his face tensed slightly when he spoke and they fought to knit his eyebrows together.

He tried to transfer the reaction to his hands, by rubbing them and looking elsewhere.

"Well good luck to you. Pleasant journey." I smiled, looked him in the eye then went on my way.

But attempting to get some distance between us without triggering more suspicion, only caused him to advance twice as fast.

"Not so fast!" He kept up with my pace. "Please tell me how to leave here!" It was a command, with considerably more bass in is voice,

"Unfortunately, all who enter here must learn for themselves." It wasn't a lie, the only way was from experience, not that I cared to lie to him anyway.

Besides, the way I entered into the folds was through the

use of my mrkb. I seriously doubted he possessed that ability.

*Although it is only a guess of mine, I don't think he entered here by his own will. No, not at all.*

And if he did figure out I was lying, fine. That would be sure to push his buttons and get him angry, angry enough for the webs to take him.

*Beyond his alien appearance, something doesn't sit right with this creature.*

"Are you toying with me?" His eyebrows suddenly became menacing—the whites of his eyes now blood red. "You *will* tell me now!" Shaking his fist, he glided in front of me and blocked my way.

I willed my body away from his a comfortable distance and I relaxed myself: releasing any tension triggered by his act.

"You are going to be in here quite awhile, if you cannot accept my words," I said as calmly as I could.

His arm came out at me wildly. Claw-like nails raked the air and barely missed me. The response I expected did not happen–– by this time he should have been swarmed by webs.

But he wasn't.

Another swing tore at my pants but did not contact skin. He scowled at me and barred dripping canines that elongated as his mouth swung open. Murderous intent filled the air between us and still nothing from the webs!

*What's going on?*

When his fangs got a little too close for comfort, I reflexively slapped the shit out the side of his face, knocking out his left set of canines. They floated in space for a bit before he grabbed them and franticallyshove them back into his mouth.

He howled in pain and looked at me pitifully like I owed him something.

*This is getting out of control!*

All the maneuvering had caused the rip in my abdomen to re-open. Blood leaked out into the air when I engaged my core.

In the midst of everything, I noticed one of the bright lights within the webs seemed familiar.

It was Jnfr.

Turning back to him, I caught him savoring the blood that he happened to catch with his tongue. He nervously reached his hand out to catch the next drop floating by. When it clung onto his fingers he eagerly smeared it across his lips.

After licking the last bit of it, he glared at me hungrily. *"More!"* he growled like an animal.

Without a second thought, he abruptly dove at me slow moving—but still presenting a threat. As I allowed him to close the gap between us, I watched as his muscles expanded in his freakishly slim frame.

When the right moment presented itself, I thrust my knee into his chin. Immediately I was struck with dizziness. It took more focus than I'd figured to outmatch his speed.

The jaw hung loosely from his mouth as if it had been dislocated. But most of his teeth remained intact, especially the ones for piercing. Next his eyes closed, seemingly involuntarily... then they flicked back open while his body floated away from me.

For a moment, a vacant look appeared on his face, replaced bit by bit with awareness. The buzzing and throbbing in my head passed just as he came at me again.

"I will have your *flesh!"* He screamed out, thirst in his voice.

"Like hell you will!" I answered back nonchalantly, finally giving up on the idea that the webs would come to my aid.

*Besides, I'm only fooling myself. If things go on this way, he* will *have my flesh.*

By this time he had to know that my injuries had slowed me down and forced me to try to distract him in our conversation. His awareness of all these things showed in the subtle shift in his behavior.

And what stood out the most, was that it appeared to escalate after he partook of my blood. Then just as quick as his energy was erratic, it plummeted and his body deflated — in an instant becoming pensive.

As if nothing happened before, he coyishingly moved closer to me, while slyly wiping his drooling mouth.

*Animals drool like that when they're starved, ready to tear at flesh and feed off whatever they come in contact with... nerves, organs and muscle...anything.*

His movement grew slow and almost rhythmatic. My body reacted by following lazingly along... and caused me to become so relaxed that I offered my arm him! He lunged at me, not caring that he was drooling more than before and that his body started to puff up once more.

But, in the midst of all that, there was a subtle humming sound in the background that I became aware of. It was foreign to me and that unfamiliarity took me out whatever spell I was in.

The lingering sound went from a faint hum in the background to an irritating pressure beating in my head.
My hand that awaited his touch quickly became a clenched fist that bashed him dead in his nose.

When I drew back I made sure to rake his eyes and just happened to catch some of his dripping blood on my fingers. They felt like they were dipped quickly in acid, I flicked off as much as I could before it burned deep.

While he worked to gather his wits, Jnfr's presence called out to me. Despite the rising inflammation of my wounds that worked hard to re-seal each time I ripped them back open, I focused desperately to propel myself away from him.

Pushing against the resistance created by the lack of gravity I strained my body, but I to move fast enough to get away from him. I eased my mind from the task of moving my body and allowed myself to drift the rest of the way to the light.

The light within the honeycomb of webs bulged out at me then drew back into itself... Engaging my mrkb swirling patterns of skhm gathered within my heart and pushed out through the surface of my chest.

My love for Jnfr was the motivating force that fed its motion, as it raised to the same vibrational range of the light and thoughts emitting from it.

Bringing the rest of my body to the same beat and rhythm, a portal slowly opened up within the center of the projected light.

Although it was opening, it wasn't happening fast enough. And that was a problem, because I sensed that thing was coming up behind me. There was no need to turn around to see that he was—the air pressure behind me began to swell in and spiral.

It was as if it was drilling into my back.

Out of panic, I grabbed the sides of the portal and tried to wrench it open wider. Pushing pass the creeping anxiety of leaving my back exposed, I strained my shoulders until it was wide enough to squeeze my body through.

A burning awareness slammed into the base of skull followed by an icy feeling.

*Shit, shit. How did he catch up so fast?!*

I dove through head first, ignoring a sudden jolt of pain spreading throughout my spine. Immediately after my body was all the way in, I looked back to see he was aiming some sort of shiny hand-held tool at me. A flash of light burst forth from a small hole at the end of what looked like a short pipe. The portal closed rapidly.

*"You must leave something behind."* It was father speaking.

*Where was he all this time?*

*"That is the way it is done."* He finished, then cut communication.

*I did. I left that thing behind.*

Everything was still, as if frozen in time, yet there was nothing here. It was like being in The Fold except there was just bright light. No way to judge distance at all. Although the weightlessness was not the same as the fold.

Then suddenly, I was paralyzed from head to toe and pulled from the core of my body. The nothingness around me coiled in and spun into a vortex that swept me in.

A force I could not identify propelled me at such a fast rate that my skin began to flap.

To protect myself from further injury, I held my abdomen together with my hands. There was no way I could curl into fetal position because bending forward stung every part of my back.

*Something happened to it when that creature aimed his tool at me... he somehow burned me. And where did he get it from?*

My body was tossed around like a ragdoll while being pulled through, and my arms became numb from the pain after being banged against the walls. Eventually a light at the end of the tunnel blazed so bright that it made no difference.

Suddenly I was spat out the opening, then splashed down into a pool of water. Besides the brunt of the impact nearly shattering my bones, all of my wounds opened further.

At first the water was mildly cold but then became unbearable. The chill sunk into all my pores then my bones — so much so the sensation grew to be hot.

## N

Despite the excruiating pain, I tried to swim to the top but some force kept me under. As I fought against the unknown entity, my skin was randomly pierced by something equally unknown... something like needles attached to tubes.

I couldn't see what it was because of the lack of light, but I still fought as hard as I possibly could against it.

The stressed air that I held in my lungs, escaped in rapid streams of bubbles. Water pumped uncontrollably into my mouth and panic set in.

*I can't breathe! I can't move...!*

When the last bit of oxygen left, I stopped struggling and floated limply. *The Fold and my father will soon have me as more than a guest...*

Suddenly I was able to breathe!

Air entered my bloodstream, and the ability to move my limbs returned. Although the range was dictated by the many needles stuck in my body. Bit by bit a medium pitch set of notes filled my ears.

It was then I knew it was Mu.

I sent back the continuation of the scale and then gave into Mu's will.

We'd never officially met, thought Jnfr often bragged about how advanced her house program was to others whenever she got a chance.

Mu released endorphins in my brain allowing me to let go even deeper. My eyes were able to see about the pool after a few jolts from our connection. Immediately I saw Jnfr's naked body surrounded by rotating rings of energy.

Besides those things spinning at an intense speed, her body was swaddled in a translucent material that seemed to be wrapped tightly around and kept her bound.

Waves of force rippled out from her location, along with a red mist like dust, that evaporated after a few feet away from her. It looked as if it was being drawn from out her body.

*Did she contract The Fever?*

Her arms began to claw away at the material that bound her, breaking up the rotation of the rings. The material regenerated itself and stifled her movement as the rings resumed their gyration.

She shuddered within the boundaries that restricted her and tried to scream out. But nothing escaped from Jnfr's mouth.

When I tried to swim over to her, I found myself unable to move far. The small distance covered allowed me to see the tears float off from her face. Tears that stayed whole without dissolving into Mu's mass.

*Jnfr must be suffering from a heavy traumatic event that caused Mu to go into action.*

Mu did not want me to interfere with its work, its desire was to keep me in one spot and out the way. Meanwhile, it attended to my wounds: extracting infection and pulling together ripped areas of flesh. It kept the flow of endorphins pumping enough to keep me sedated without getting me too high.

I ran my hands across the freshly made keloid which decreased in swelling. Whatever remained would be a constant reminder of this day.

Looking at Jnfr bound and unconscious, I wondered what she endured this day, to end up like this. Maybe accessing Mu's records of the house would tell me.

With the use of the eye, I reached into Jnfr's mind to connect to Mu's program. What I found surprised me. She possessed an eye as well— one she'd received just recently.

Although accessing her mind directly would have provided all the answers, I intuitively knew it would be dangerous for the both of us.

Once I found the membrane that connected Jnfr and Mu, I sent a light range of notes that were immediately answered by heavy chords.

Mu was resisting. Looking to brush me aside it sent

heavier chords that caused a sharp migraine, But I persisted until the whole tag of war began to affect Jnfr's mind.

Upon seeing that it was contributing to Jnfr being unstable, and that I would not let go, Mu allowed me access... A landslide of watery images shot across my mind literally flushing out any newly forming ones.

It was aggressive and totally controlled by Mu— like it was being an asshole about the whole thing. I quickly utilized the eye, noticing that I was becoming better at grounding, myself and streaming the images to a slower rate.

After a time, I found the stretch of waves I was searching for.

Her mother had transitioned earlier today, her depature was pushed by Dvln, Rkm's father.

*But who was that little girl that receieved one of the eyes? What is her role in any of this?*

Determined to console Jnfr no matter what it took, I yanked out the tubes from my skin and swam over to her. Mu did nothing to prevent me, yet it did cut access.

Before I made it over to her, one large burst of red light shot out from her. She shook violently the rings responded by closing in, though they had a difficult time keeping her still.

Her eyes flew open and she started yell. But nothing could

be heard underwater... bubbles of air poured to the surface. Once awake, she frantically tore at the material once more which triggered stronger constriction.

I reached in a gap between the heavy spinning just—barely getting my arm pulled out the socket. Holding her hand, I stroked her fingers to calm her down, her skin was on fire. It was then I saw remnants of the link with Mu fluttering about in my thoughts,

Before I tried to pull it in, it opened to me and allowed me a deeper access than before to Jnfr. Shrouds of murky spirit force, formed dense wall outside her consciousness. It was The Fever.

Mu augmented my focus and together we hammered at the barrier and caused the bonds within its structure to waver. We struck once again and burst through its shell. I continued on to her consciousness while Mu thoroughly denatured whatever bits of protein sought to re-combine.

In doing so, it managed to remove what actually anchored itself to her being.

*"Jnfr, it's okay... You can stop now."* I sent to her gently.

*"Kvn. Kvn is that you? What—"* She stopped in mid-sentence.

Gradually the rings dissolved into the water along with the material wrapped around Jnfr's body. She was now able to move freely now, and laid a hand on my face... running her fingers across my chin.

Mu interrupted us when it embraced us both and brought us out. It gently rolled us out of a small wave and onto the edge of the pool.

It took me a moment to breathe air directly rather than extracting oxygen from the water. After I finished coughing up the last bit of water from my lungs, I turned to face Jnfr; who was staring at me the whole time. She shuffled over to me and buried her head into my chest.

Her wooly wet hair rubbed across my soaked shirt and the coarseness of her hair that bristled through it. It was a comfort.

"Your mother…" I spoke without thinking. "She is fine."

It was then that I realized the impact my visit to The Fold had left on me. Now that I had a moment free of anxiety, I was able to focus on the throbbing in my head.

The nagging impressions calling forth images of both our parents finally began to thin out. Not just their images, but the actual *imprint.*

Their essences were talking to me by stimulating biochemical discharges.

"You've seen her?" Jnfr questioned, wanting to believe me without asking.

"I feel her." It was as if they were both as part of me, as my own thoughts. "The impression of her essence are in my cells along with my father's... He transitioned as well."

Jnfr's face became sunken. The light in her eyes dimmed and her lids fell. Then the atmosphere became thick and a hazy heat grew, yet it was pleasant. Her dismal eyes disappeared with a rapid jerk of her eyelids. She batted her eyes as if she was waking up from a dream. Everything about us was blanketed in heat, except for the cold floor: which brought its own pleasant feeling before it took in the constant generation of warmth into its fibers.

Mu who had been watching us the whole time from the pool, briskly withdrew as Jnfr suddenly looked at it.

Jnfr started to gasp for air clutching at her chest while she propped herself up with her other hand. My own breathing became irregular as well and I was becoming aroused.

It was happening beyond our control. We were going to unite.

"Jnfr did you feel that…that humming in your chest?" I spoke between rapid breaths.

"Yes, I can't but help to feel it." She paused as her breath lightly escaped out her mouth. "But it's not happening in my chest." She looked at me hungrily, her eyes filled with a wanting.

Then smiled, baring her teeth.

"Is it happening? Are we…" She stopped abruptly as her cheeks became red, the blood of desire filling.

In that moment—as if she just remembered that she was naked—she tried to cover herself with her arms.

However, all the hugging did nothing but squeeze out water from her between her breasts and from between her legs, leaving my imagination to roam back to the source of where the drips leaked from.

Whatever look she saw on my face made her scamper back from me— doing her best not to turn her body to expose her best parts.

"Are you serious? What's with all this sudden shyness?" I demanded.

"Stay back!"

She spoke as if I were a stranger, a stranger that she was overwhelming attracted to; judging by the amount of excited vapor and light that escaped her body.

Jnfr did a good job controlling what came out of her mouth, but she wasn't able to refrain from the subtle seductive changes in her posture...

The arching of her back and the subtle gyration of her hips across the floor...the way she, every so often, licked her lips, biting them just as her tongue went back into her mouth... and the steady fluctuation of pheromones in the air almost created a misty wall between us.

*Yet, her scent is different...it is more than her natural body odor, the ingrained aroma of the forest and the herbs she works with. Yes something is definitely...*

"Different. Your scent is not the same." She blurted, at the same time I thought it.

"Yours too. And the funny thing is that I want you more than ever."

Jnfr shuddered, and inched back further away from me when my words finished. Then without warning, she leapt on top of me, nervously pinned my shoulder to the floor and straddled my legs together.

I nimbly reached out for her, still winded by my back being slammed into the floor. She pounded her hands into my biceps. My arms immediately went weak and fell as she imposed her weight.

"Now its my turn," she whispered anxiously into my ear, drawing back her voice on the last word.

The scent she emitted drove me crazy and left me weak at the same time. She had the advantage. The timid energy in her behavior was gone.

My heart fluttered, reacting to the images that ran vividly in my head of what she may be planning next. Jnfr left my arms go and reached for the bottom of my shirt. Bit by bit she pulled the shirt up my body and then over my head. She unloosened my pants and yanked them off my legs.

When it came to my underwear she hesitated. She'd never seen me naked before. She fumbled about a bit before she peeled me out of them.

"This is no fun," she said disappointedly.

"No *fun?"* I answered defensively. I was more than willing to defend the fact that it was fun and that we should keep on.

"Yes, no fun. You're just laying there like a lifeless doll."

"Wait a minute! I almost transitioned twice today and received my father's eyes without the ritual. I'm drained. Damn. At least my mt still can stand," I protested.

She laughed.

"You find that funny?" Now I was irritated.

"No I don't." She changed her demeanor and got serious. "I just meant that I want you to touch me too. Hold me."

I turned away ashamed. She lifted my head back so I could see her face. When our eyes met the intensity of her focus leaked skhm out her eyes, the heat flowing off it touched my face.

She shifted with her head from side to side like a cat, never taking her eyes off me. The heat from her glare wiped across my face with the motion of her neck. As her eyebrows gradually unknitted, her grip relaxed. She leaned in closer. Not once did she blink, her skhm pushed into mind. And soon I was aware of what she was really doing to me.

A mild migraine ran through my head leaving in its path a cool sensation. Along with that, something was being lifted by layer in my thoughts, with each layer I felt a little at ease.

When she came to the last layer, I started to pull away from her. I resisted pushing back looking to drive her skhm away. She smiled.

Then unexpectantly she pressed her supple lips against mine, pushing her tongue in between them... she licked my lips until I opened my mouth. As our tongues enjoyed the feeling of one another, swirling about and increasing the current of electricity... she then delicately lifted the last layer without any fight from me.

When the occasional erratic breaths we took through our nose weren't enough— we sucked on each others forcing our skin to do more work. We pawed each other like wild animals, stimulated by each near transition experience from drawing recklessly upon our nkh force.

"Take from me whatever you wish..." Jnfr sung out; breaking our connection to speak.

The dimmed Tkkn in the corners withdrew from its green hue and flickered into a luminescent indigo.

"I want you Kvn." She roughly jerked her body and rolled us over so that I would be on top.

What was strange was all I could do was gaze at her, amidst this perfect setting for us to unite. My thoughts were far from the groping I planned to do when this time came.

"All I want is to be one with you," I said with hesitance.

Jnfr gently laid a hand on my cheek then let it slip brushing across my face. "So do I and the journey there is into my cave."

What she said scared the shit out of me. I was never so nervous about doing something, that I was so longing to do.

"That's right Kvn." There was a sarcastic tone in voice, she raised her hand and placed it on top of my head. "Let's see what's really behind all that mess you talk." She was serious.

"I…" my throat was like sand.

"You what?" Jnfr stared at me then rolled her eyes and tapped her fingers on her cheek.

I clumsily threw her legs up over my shoulders and fumbled about trying to put my mt inside her.

"You did that backwards, let me help..." She was calm—

too calm, especially for the skhm carrying her intentions off her body.

She took hold of my mt and rubbed it around her lips before taking it inside of her. She was so wet and warm, that I wanted to thrust until I exploded... not go about it easy.

When my shoulder tensed up and contracted all other surrounding muscles, she stopped and looked at me with concern.

"If you do that…you will join your father." She meant it.

Although I enjoyed the roughness of the first few strokes, it made me curious about what thrusting into her would be like. I followed her lead yet struggled with the thought of it.

A small amount of blood trickled out of her womb and onto my leg, I nervously pulled out of her.

"Why did you do that?" She asked irritatingly.

"Blood…you're bleeding!"

"It will pass." She assured me,

She gently wrapped her smooth wet legs around my back then aggressively kicked her heels into it. With hardly any effort, she was able to send a strong enough jolt for me to thrust my pelvis forward out of surprise.

The walls of her womb spread apart as my mt roughly parted them. She heaved heavily at the chest and let out long soft moans, and it seemed her juices followed along with the rhythm making our journey together...exquisite.

Eventually our hips stopped competing for dominance and fed off of the shared ebb and flow of the strokes. As the last stroke drove in deeper than the one before, sending out a gush of juices, suddenly I could not sense my mt, only something pushing into my pelvis.

"Why can't I feel you?" Jnfr began to panic. "What's happening?" She struggled to get me off of her but something in me resisted and beckoned for me to stay mounted on her.

"GET *OFF!"* Her voice rode out her mouth like a slap carrying skhm.

She swung wildly at my face without hesitation or second thought, her eyes glared at me like a beast ready to kill. One of her barrage of punches got through and connected the boniest knuckle on her fist with the hinge of my jaw.

It took everything I had in me to remain conscious and flow with it as my neck whipped sharply. I let out all of my breath and spat up to the side the foul taste in mouth to stop from vomiting.

Before she had a chance to land another blow, I hugged her as tight as I could and lifted her from off the floor. Sitting myself upright, I picked her body up and sat her on top of my mt. She struggled to get free, no longer enjoying the moment of our union.

And although a part of me was put off by what naturally came to me and what was causing her discomfort, I kept on driving into her. After a few moments, her mouth opened wide and let out a satisfying groan.

Her body went limp and swayed freely side to side, as the back of her hands slapped a rhythm into my legs. Still I felt nothing in my mt, regardless of my legs covered in her juices and sweat.

Yet there was a something steadily pulsing in the middle of my chest and between my eyebrows. A pulsation that was orgasmic and caused me to pant heavy.

"K-K-v-n-n-n, I feel nothing in my womb! but my chest and head feels sooo good!" She spurted, attempting to catch her breath.

The whites of her eyes first became bloodshot followed by a strange glow as the middle of them contracted.

"Kvn what's happening to your eyes?" She spoke in surprise yet faint.

"Something is happening to yours too!" I could not hold back my anxiety.

## N

A rushing sound swept through my ears, as if everything other sound was drained out from the room by it. Jnfr lips moved but I heard no words come out and despite all this I continued to stroke into her womb.

A part of me was scared out my mind, so I thought that as long as I stayed connected with her I wouldn't be alone. A light-headed sensation coursed through me following a frightful numbness in all my limbs. Then I was left with only an awareness of a small humming rising.

*Am I leaving my body?* This was too much to handle. *I can't take all these heavy trips between realms.* Helplessly I watched my body jerk about and experienced no physical connection as I hovered over it.

Then warmth was near me.

But how could I feel warmth now?

I turned around and saw Jnfr floating there next to me.

She had a soft flowing glowing astral-like body with no distinguishable facial features, yet I still recognized her.

When I reached out to her, I drew back with surprise to see my own hand float about with the same glowing astral like mist and then...

## *Chapter Medju Khemenu*
## *Your Life, Like Mine*

I eagerly reached out for his hand as he drew it away. I needed his touch—otherwise I would just fade away.

*Just when I was getting used to the feeling of ectasy running through my chest, this happens.*

*Being in this state reminds me too much of mother, watching her transition as flesh burned away…I will never forget.*

*Never.*

Before Kvn's hand completely got away, I caught one of his fingertips. As soon as contact was made, our bodies were hurled towards one another, then merged together.

What I experienced was beyond words or thoughts, it was total unity with Kvn. Everything that tormented him this day I shared with him. And the same went for me.

Our bodies trembled in unison, as they smiled at one another then finally we reached our climax and shot life essences into and onto each other. The current generated from our ejaculations rode up our spines then into us. Everything within us tingled and exploded then sucked in and exploded again.

Our physical bodies collapsed to the floor and shivered in exctasy. Kvn was still inside of Jnfr. We watched on as one unified spirit, our physical bodies came down from the high of orgasm and collapsed onto each other.

"YOUNG ONES NOW THAT YOU HAVE BROUGHT YOUR AWARENESS TO A HEIGHTENED STATE THROUGH YOUR UNION, I AM ABLE TO SHARE WITH YOU WHAT ONLY A FEW ARE PRIVY TO."

A distant yet familiar voice spoken from no particular place, each of its words seamed into our being and spread into every part. And at the same time all things around us spoke the same words from their cores.

We reached out to the eyes of our parents that lay within our limp and sexually satiated bodies. We peered deeply into the walls of our blood and the recent impressions made into Kvn's memories from our parents.

*The All Nature. We are being spoken to directly by the Mother of All.*

"QUIET YOURSELVES AND LISTEN. SOON I, YOUR WORLD, WILL BE LOCKED IN WHAT YOU MAY CALL A COMPETITION. A COMPETITION WITH OTHER WORLDS TO DETERMINE POSITION IN OUR HOUSES."

We wanted to speak to the All Nature directly but we were so awe struck the lips of our thoughts fell numb.

"A FEW SOULS ON MY SURFACE WILL REPRESENT US ALL, YOU ARE A PART OF THAT GROUP. YOU WILL FIGHT FOR OUR POSTION."

"I NEED YOU TO FIND THESE TWO."

An image of Nth streamed across our consciousness followed by one of Drrn.

"BE SWIFT IN FINDING THEM. ONE MORE THING. BEINGS FROM ONE OF THE WORLDS I AM IN COMPETITION WITH HAVE MADE THEIR WAY TO MY SURFACE."

"PLEASE DEAL WITH THIS ONE THAT GOT STUCK IN MY FOLDS."

*What beings?*

The sway of the air and skhm in the room gathered and swirled close to where we lay. A vacuum formed near our bodies, all about us there was a heavy drawing in of energies.The force was so strong it surprisingly tugged at our forms as it seeped into our own space.

While we struggled to keep every part of our astral bodies from floating off into its almost alluring pull, the small patch of air collapsed in on itself. A portal into The Fold appeared in the tear then roughly spewed out that creature we'd encountered earlier.

As soon as the pale body hit the wood floor, the tear sealed itself instantly, leaving no trace of the disruption it caused. His tumbling came to an abrupt halt when he slammed into the wall. As soon as his arms slumped to the floor, he leapt up and darted for our bodies.

He scrambled across the floor on all fours like a predator, deftly pushed Jnfr's chin in one direction then pulled her shoulder in the opposite. Jnfr's limp body gave way to his prodding, her neck locked into place then released a light scent of musk into the air.

Not knowing how to release ourselves from our state, we helplessly watched him revel in the sexual energy that enveloped the room.

Her vessels throbbed to the surface of her skin while his eagerness expressed itself in thick drool that poured out over it. His naked body poised over her's caused us much distress!

Just before his gaping mouth pushed his fangs in, Mu's watery mass forcefully sprung from out the pool and took hold of his legs. It dangled him upside down from the ceiling until his face became red as blushfruit from the rush of blood that flooded it, then it released him.

His skull awkwardly struck against the floor and cracked sharply... followed by the rest of him sprawled out across the floor.

Mu didn't give him time to recover, she snatched him up again— repeating the same thing like a cat toying with a mouse. Over and over, Mu used his head like a hammer until his agonizing screams blended into the snapping sound of floorboards.

Once it was satisfied that the threat was diminished, Mu withdrew its waters, leaving his small pale frame bruised and purple, crumpled up amidst a pile broken wood—breathing erractically, unconscious but barely alive.

Mu then shifted its attention to our inert bodies and lifted them from the floor, bringing them to stand. Then, without warning, it sent an astral-like stream into the place where we were suspended. With meticulous precision it swathed our bodies in its waters, and easily drew us out.

The gaseous bonds that kept us bound in this plane gently gave way and released their hold on us. Mu carefully split our beings, peeling apart the interwoven layers of our essences and re-encoding their helixes.

Emotionally we were dissolved from our unity, yet an underlying subtle link was deeply rooted into our essences.

*I feel like myself again, but he is as near to me as my own breath.*

Mu placed us back into our perspective bodies and as I became re-acquainted with my limbs, a sense of ease filled every cell in my body.

The Fever was gone.

The cold air in the room wrapped itself around my naked body. I couldn't help but to shiver as I stood in front of Kvn, who igrnored my erected nipples and stared straight into my eyes.

I was no longer shy about my body. I ran my hands up the sides of it and gasped. The warm luscious stimulations took hold of my thoughts. I hugged myself and trembled as more of my erotic juices burst through my lips and slid down between my legs.

I turned and looked at Kvn who seemed to be watching

me the whole time...grinning.

"What are you looking at?" I barked at him doing my best to hold in my jubilation.

"Oh nothing...I gotcha *now!*" He answered me as if he conquered me or something...and he had.

*But I conquored him too.*

"Skhmt!" I called out to my sturdier outfit, so that I would be clothed... there was still that pale creature to contend with.

"Show off!" Kvn said, a little enviously.

He had to put his clothes by hand. He lacked the training in Hn Arts. And it seemed that regardless of the enhancement of the eye, somethings did not come naturally.

As soon as we were both dressed, I took Kvn by the hand and squeezed lightly. "Look, I know you had little to no experience with Hn, but you are going to have to take a crash course."

"Okay, what do I do?"Kvn sounded determined to learn. "You can direct Hn to do many things especially with the use of the eye." I explained to him.

"First bring your attention to your eye." I instructed .

"Got it." Kvn answered.

"Now extend that attention to your clothes. See it in your mind... your... eye make your clothing an extension of yourself."

"I'm trying." he strained himself, closed his eyes and made faces. "There is something in the way..." He continued to strain until the floor beneath us tremored a little.

Mu became startled out of its repair and started towards Kvn.

"Stop Mu." I used the eye instead of my implants, it was quicker, Mu stopped just before it attacked Kvn.

Kvn was still struggling with contacting the Hn and was oblivious to what just happened.

"Kvn," he kept on. "Kvn!"my yell jogged him out his fervour.

*"What?"* he snapped at me; he was upset

"You are driving away the Hn of the fabric. It is resisting you because you are trying to force your way in." I explained, and placed my hand gently on his face.

He let the tension that distorted his face relax which also lifted the awareness of Mu.

"Do it again. Without the intensity of before... Touch your sleeve without using you hand." I motioned to my eye and then sleeve of my own outfit. He did it again, calmly waves of Hn energy blanketed his body.

Suddenly, the pale child's arm— grabbing our attention.

Kvn skulked towards the pale child, he was twisting near the newly formed floorboards Mu just finished creating.

"Kvn?" I called out to him, slightly fearful.

He didn't answer.

Kvn cautiously squatted down in front of the child, a strange looking creature that reminded me of Nth except for the total lack of color of his skin.

"I have seen nothing like him on this world. Even worst up close..." He said.

Kvn placed his hand on that thing's neck and pulled back in shock, his face scrunched up in disgust. He tried to calm himself down, but only made himself excited the more he talked.

"His skin is like mush, no strength to it. And cold, no heat. How could something like that *be?*"

I squinted my eye to activate my perception and projected it towards him. My eye skimmed over the energy he emitted and his structure. What Kvn said was right.

*He is an adult, much older than us—there is a certain air of maturity about him.*

The deeper I allowed my eye to peer the more his nature was revealed.

His heart-rate pounded rapidly, none of his beats followed

a specific rhythm they followed a scattered drum. He was out cold, and it was as if his heart struggled to supply his cells with blood.

"Look at this." Kvn held up his small hand between his pinky and index finger. "Damn, his arm is heavy like lead!"

Kvn seemed to struggle to keep holding it up. Flesh slightly tore away between Kvn's grip and the rest of his hand.

I could practically see out the other side of his arm—the translucent hue of his grayish-pink skin was like a window to his strained looking vessels burdened by circulation. We turned to one another nervously, Kvn had a look of disgust on his face.

"Let him go!" I screamed out to him then turned up my face.

"Shit!" He cussed angrily, dropped the hand and then vigorously brushed off the string of flesh hanging from his fingers. "We need to get this thing out of here." He said dropping his head and rubbing the back of his neck.

"Mu..." I called.

Mu, in its humanoid form, arrived at the side of the creature in a matter seconds in response from my mental cue. It scooped up the body, momentarily stopped to recalibrate its density to hold its weight and prevent it from slipping out its grasp; then disappeared behind the flaps.

"Jnfr." Kvn said in a dry yet serious in tone. "Whatever we are about to face..."

He paused then hands covered his face with his hands. He slid his fingers down to his chin, and grabbed at the small bit of hair on the tip of it.

"It may be like the one Mu took out of here. I won't let any of them touch you." The strength of his words shook me where I stood and he meant every last one of them. It was as if my entire being was held safely in his arms.

"Now let me see…"

He looked intently at the sleeves of his shirt. Bit by bit the material pulled tighter together and strengthened its fibers. It drew in the skhm from the air and constructed extra layers of fabric around his joints and neck.

His footwear wove halfway up his lower leg and expanded the soles. He cut short his focus and coughed uncontrollably before he was able to catch his breath. By that time I already honed in on the signal he emitted to the Hn in his clothing and duplicated its frequency.

I sent the duplicated talk into my own clothing, making slight alterations in its rate here and there. Kvn nodded his head with approval once I was done.

His eyes and head worked together beaming in on my

accentuated breasts and hips.

"Mmmmm..." He let out a low moan running his hands down my sides.

"So where is it?" He asked right out the blue bringing us both back to the matter at hand.

Meanwhile, the whole time he poked around in my mind to find out so he didn't have to ask me again Kvn. We did need to get going to find Nth and my father.

A few drops of water leaked from the ceiling and onto my forehead.

"Mu took that thing outside to leave for the animals."

"And?"

"It woke up and somehow got free from Mu then ran off in the woods." Kvn balled up his fist and scowled his face.

"Mu put up the house field as soon as he disappeared in the distance. He won't be able to get back in."

Kvn's fist went loose along with the sigh of relief held in his chest.

"Come."

I took Kvn by the hand while he continue to probe for a location. I let it out to him to build his confidence in his skill. "I know where it is."

Now he arrogantly strode ahead of me then pulled me

along by my wrist, I didn't resist him and he still nearly dragged me.

When we got to the edge of the pool he stared at the rippling surface then at me. Brushing off his anxiety, I cleared my throat and raised my arms above the water then slapped my palms together.

I pressed in on them until they caused me to tremble, slowly the water followed my movement.

*It's been awhile since I'd used this technique, actually I was showed only once but wasn't allowed to since.*

The heat in my palms coursed into my arms then rushed into my chest. In my mind, I said the one word mother taught me from young, the word that I only knew.

My name.

The folds in my vocal cords swelled up with the heat from my chest and the stream of my name from my thoughts.

In the voice that mother taught me to use, I released it in the air from my lungs and breathed it onto the surface of the pool. Before long a whirlpool appeared in the center, it drew in my essence and mixed it into every part of itself. I caught Kvn looking my breasts jiggle out the corner of my eye.

"So this is how you imprinted your essence into the house, huh?" Kvn asked while making no secret of where his eyes held their attention.

"Why not just use a master Tkkn and save more time?" He folded his arms and tapped his fingers.

"We live in the woods and with the flow of time here, what time would we be saving?" I asked him simply. *There's no need to speak in depth about things he doesn' know.*

I pulled apart my hands and the water followed along by dividing equally and revealing a path to the opposite of the pool…to an archway and door.

"Let's go Kvn."

This time I lead the way; I could tell by the puzzled look on Kvn's face that he was lost. I jumped down into the path and he reluctanctly leapt in behind.

As we neared the other end, he looked from side to side at the flowing water being held at bay by the force I generated, intermittedly he jerked his neck when he felt that water would come crashing in on him.

*It's not that the water is going to come crashing in on him, he is sensing the intention of the water responding to his fear.*

"Have you learned anything at all?" I asked.

"No." He dropped his head. "Can we talk about that later?" He wanted to change the subject.

Annoyance filled his voice, he dragged his feet across the

smooth floor and pulled away from me in our link. That was enough for me to drop it.

"Place your hand on the door." I motioned to the stone surface of the door in the archway.

"Why?" Now he wanted to be difficult.

"The water that has been stirring up at our sides will come crashing in on us if I don't make you known to the Hn beyond this door."

He smirked and lazily raised his arm up and wiggled his fingers before he slapped his hand heavy on the stone.

*"ARRRRRGHHHHH!"* Kvn screamed out in pain and dropped to his knees, his arms flailed about— striking at the walls of water disrupting the barrier.

Whatever struck Kvn, had struck me as blunt as it did him. Something filled my mind, a presence, hammering on my thoughts taking their space.

Curled up in ball and rolling around next to Kvn, I desperately rubbed the sides of my head seeing that is it also took hold of the muscles around my skull and constricted them.

"I GAVE YOU FORM, FOR YOUR LIFE ON MY SURFACE, MY WORDS ARE NOT TO BE TAKEN LIGHTLY. "

"NOW THAT I HAVE YOUR ATTENTION. FIND

THIS WOMAN." The All Nature finished its words and returned our senses back to us…but not before it scraped across the eyes of our brains the image of Nth.

Kvn struggled to get himself up then humbly approached the door and placed his palm to it. I still sat on the ground, reeling from the effects, yet not making much of it.

I watched Kvn's openly shaken behavior... then questioned whether or not I was still normal.

"Kvn?" He didn't respond. "Kvn!" I said a little louder to break the daze he was in as he stared at the door. Nothing.

"KVN!" I yelled in his mind. He jumped in shock and snapped his head in my direction.

"WHAT?" He screamed back at me yet managed not to remove his hand from the door.

"Open your mind to me." I said calmly.

Reluctantly what little bit of pitiful shields that still remained around him melted away, once the pulse of his thoughts became visible I wasted no time seizing it.

The second I fed that pulse into the Hn connected to the door, he slammed his free hand against the door and howled out.

Kvn had no Hn training only combat training. It was plain to see that he is traumatized by the receiving of the eye from his father.

"What's happening?" he said in panic, paralyzed just like I was by what we were witnessing.

His hand began to take on the skin of the rock, and patiently scraped out a gravel grinding sound during its transition. Beautiful smooth brown skin gave way to course and dense rock.

"Don't move." I called out softly.

My growing fear of his entire body merging with the Hn consciousness in the door could not be seen on my face. I did my best to keep a plain expression.

Although I knew something was going to happen, I had no choice but to go ahead with it regardless of his suffering.

*No way did I think it would be like this— his essence is being absorbed.*

"Jnfr you better fix this…now!" Kvn bellowed out.

He did his best to remain still as the petrification climbed up his arm. Beads of sweat blanketed his forehead and when he shuddered the drops struck his chest.

*None remain there for long before being consumed by his clothing.*

"Jnfr..." he pleaded.

"I can't feel my hand." He screamed out.

"Stay still." *Oh no!* "This is normal." There was nothing

normal about this, but I had to say *something.*

*What makes matters worst is the slow encroachment of the walls, ever since the door began assimilating him— another thing I kept from Kvn.*

*What can I do? I am unsure if we can take another beating from The All Nature for hesitating from this point on.*

*If I use Mu that would short circuit the house and send the walls crushing in on us.*

"What are you doing?' His voice was low almost lifeless.

I placed my hand on his and forced my blood out my vessels through my pores and onto his stone-skin. The petrification stopped right before his elbow, then withdrew back down his arm, his own brown-skin returned like the ebb of a wave leaving sand.

My palm was on fire, thousands of pores vented their disgust with me while they unwillingly and painfully fed his hand the imprints within my blood.

It was over.

With his hand returned to normal, a glimmer of strength appeared on his face until he saw his thumb.

"What the…" he clutched at his newly feminine digit and clenched his jaw tight.

"I…" what could I say.

He scorned his thumb for a few moments then wound it in material, increased its layers then molded it to the shape of his left thumb.

"What now?" he was calm although I could tell he is still pissed.

I drew in a deep breath until the air pressure contacted my womb. "Mmmmmmmmmmmmmmm...!"

The energy spiraled up through my kidneys and into my spinal cord. The skhm gushed upwards and flushed out the stagnate energy in my vertebrae then finally spread over my head like a hood.

The gathered skhm pushed on the circulation in my eyes then beamed from out their cells and blanketed the surface of the door. Minute pieces of granite that was held firm together distanced themselves from each other.

"Why are those pieces of stone following my movement?" Kvn asked curiously and swayed side to side noticing how the bits of stone mirrored his movement.

"Stay still."

On my last word, hundreds of small stones flew out at us in thousands of small pieces, and covered us from head to toe.

"We can enter now." I motioned to the thin field of stone in front of us.

Our bodies easily passed into the shield and out the other side since we were recognized by the Hn within. Otherwise our flesh and bone would of got stuck in between the space of granite then eventually crushed as they were brought back together.

After a few steps, we heard the crashing of the halves of water from beyond the door followed by the grind of stone.

I remembered vaguely the narrow dark corridor ahead of us, its passageway lit by what lay behind the white quartz walls to our sides. Kvn, without thinking, reached out for the walls then nervously drew back.

"What are those blue globes of light? How many are there? " He stopped, looking at the endless rows of illuminated globes of light.

"Those are Mu's children. They become the Mother when one Mu is at the end of their cycle."

"I see. No wonder it is so damp here and at the same time full of life," he commented while moving sluggishly with his garment of stone.

By the time we reached the end of the corridor, most of our little escorts already returned to the door. Kvn shook his body out and sighed in relief.

"There it is Kvn." I pointed to what Kvn was nosing

around for earlier.

"Who made this? It looks custom." He said in excitement as he ran his hand along its body.

"Mother did. Every last detail put in by her own hands."

"Why did she never joined a guild? She would have been a Master Guildsman with no difficulty," he said admiringly reaching for the driving controls.

"Don't touch that!" I pushed him away before he made contact and caused us more delay.

"You really don't know much do you?" I said without restraint.

Kvn seemed upset and almost distant while I was speaking to him. He seemed to be hiding something. I could poke around without his knowing to find out.

"I don't," he interrupted me just before I started to probe his thoughts. "So you'll have to teach me." He smiled.

"Let's get in." I sat in the front seat on the right side and he on the left.

"Before you touch anything, you need a quick lesson."

"Right." He agreed, the tension between us in the link subsided. It was smooth.

"This vehicle you see is not like the ones you in the city," I explained holding his full attention.

"It takes more than simple Hn knowledge to operate and is fueled by more than the skhm around us."

"What else does it need?" He asked curiously.

"Your personal skhm and your Ba. My mother did not believe in idle use of our connection with the All-Nature. Anything that would be considered out of mainstream connection was not allowed," I told him.

"So when you did use that force it was definitely out of necessity and nothing more. She made sure that everything in our home was programmed the same way." As I spoke I started to really see the importance of Mother's reasoning.

*"Everything."* I stressed that point.

"That sounds like that she made sure your life was on the line anytime you used the arts," he said in shock.

"Exactly." I agreed.

"Why?" He asked, now deeply concerned about his own well-being.

"Simple. Two words. Non-elaboration and Connection."

My answer was only meant to be a seed in his thoughts. "Anyway, we just need for the vehicle to recognize you as family. Nothing more. You won't be risking your life to operate it." I kept my emotions hidden from him...along with the full truth.

He seemed relieved, the tension in our link re-appeared.

*Kvn is concerned about my well-being.*

"Bring your mind to the pumping of your heart and focus on how that pulse reaches all your cells in your body."

"That's easy enough." He said with confidence. "Now focus on the weight of that pulse flowing outward to you entire body."

"Breathe in and bring your breath to that pulse." I explained in the simplest of terms I could.

"I feel like..like." He found it difficult to explain. "Like your whole essence is one pulse, right?"

"That is your consciousness," I said. "Keep your focus on your consciousness, do not lose focus no matter what."

*And he'd better not.*

"Now place your hands into the panels on your sides," I instructed.

He slowly placed his hands into the small pools filled with gel-like liquid spheres at his sides, which we actually a part of the outer-lungs of the vehicle. The alveoli-like spheres crept up his arm to his elbow.

Kvn stood firm, almost in a trance, he was doing what he was told to do.

"Stay focused."

The vehicle rumbled a bit as it drew skhm from around us through Kvn's body, without his knowing.

"I apologize Kvn. Your life is now on the line as well."

## *Chapter Medju Pasedju*
## *The Beginning*

"How many more of you want to be with your brethren?" I pushed my voice into their ears to damage their sense of hearing and disrupt their equilibrium.

"Then come—be like them! Cold and at my feet!" I ripped off an arm of one their fallen and tossed it at where I sensed the ones huddled together.

As for the ones that lurked in the darkness, Tzkw's eye kept track of their stalking and their sekhem emissions.

The thickness of tension in the air steadily rose as their numbers increased and consumed the last bit of Apep's decayed body to materialize.

Underneath the skin of Khat, I felt the blood of the first four I encountered dry, tighten and pull on the skin of my hands. Rather than have it removed, the urge to leave it as war-marks compelled me otherwise.

Earlier on, when the sudden shift to battle took hold of the situation, they were already one step ahead of me having sensed me first. They were upon me so swiftly that I was forced to crudely rip out the throats of the first two and snap the necks of the others.

All of which happened in a flash before Khat sealed around my hands. No shouts of battle came from their lips…only viciousness.

*In the past, I found the flesh of the Alde to be like mush to extreme force— that fact has not changed.*

Once they met their end, an onslaught of less experienced fighters charged in clumsily, possibly they were still disorientated from just coming into physical being.

Nevertheless, they met their end just the same. But their bodies were heavier than in the past.

Since then, Esfet continued to escalate in the chamber and fed off the bodies littered in front of me and whatever else it could draw from.

The same way a beast would devour its prey then excrete what could not be digested, it released a stark, stale coldness into the air from its feeding.

And in some synergistic way, that feeding fueled the Alde's

intent, as they did their best to masked their movement. The heaviness of their frames made noticeable imprints in the air pressure.

Closer.

They were getting within range to strike from a distance.

"Stop!" One of them, a female in voice, called out from their ranks.

The shifting of bodies and displacement of small rocks upon the ground ceased.

She was someone in authority. Her musk was stronger than the others. The naked pale frame that stepped out from the shadows yielded sculpted slender muscles.

If not for the depth of her hips and breasts, she could easily be mistaken for a man.

"What are you doing on this world?" She spoke with some familiarity in her tone, while her kinsmen kept their bodies still.

"I am here. The rest is none of your concern." My answer came quickly and without calculation in its tone.

In my experience with them, flat outright communication always coerced information from them, despite their cunning nature. They seemed to respect non-emotional expression.

"You are," she curtly responded.

She was withholding something— the way her Ka

suddenly shifted in hostility and flooded her aura. "And you will die having sided with this world, leaving nothing left to live in future memory!"

That was all I needed to hear.

They meant to conquer this world, my Aunt Khusat.

*The thought of it momentarily took me off guard. What will happen to Jnfr? The life in my womb?* My fists tightened as my heart beat wildly. *No harm will come to them!*

Once I became aware of my heightened raise of Ka, my fingers loosened and my heart returned back to the rhythm I set it at for battle.

Quietly I sent my Ka out over the corpses to measure the distance in relation to the ones who stalked in the shadows then I sent it towards the wall behind me.

A situation like this one may appear dismal to the most experienced of Aha, for me it only awakened my lust for battle. And this time, I would take the battle to them.

Rushing forward meant exposing my back and sides to them, nevertheless that option was becoming more attractive with each passing moment.

"Well," I started off. "You have set an interesting snare at the expense of your kinsmen." I paused. "What a price to pay for un-gained quarry."

"The game has just begun." The smoothness of her voice did not land on deaf ears as she sank back in the darkness.

Several strange pulses disrupted empty space all about the chamber leaving something heavy and large in those areas. Soon after they russled about in the shadows—doing their best to cover their steps with more amateur Ka projections— silence followed.

Then nothing. Suddenly, sharp clicking sounds broke the silence— for me it was like the music of battle was rekindled. The principle of rhythm kissed my ba and my ba embraced Khat, all was in full swing.

I instantly latched my hearing onto the sounds and laid my body as flat as I could against the ground. Just as the grit of the rocky surface settled into my face, beams of light shot over my head followed by whistling bursts.

Clumps of the wall behind me crumpled down, stirred in smoke and carried the scent of scorched earth. Other clicking followed, within seconds I wedged myself in between a few of the rapidly decomposing bodies and covered up any exposed part of myself with their limbs.

When the beams hit their lifeless corpses, that literally crushed me with their weight, the aroma of burnt putrid flesh assailed my nostrils. Yet it didn't dampen my focus on how much their group's position shifted only made adversity a stronger bedmate.

Something *old*, a forgotten past feeling took hold of me...the same rush of emotions and skhm that filled me when I was first forced to protect those I loved....

Back on my beloved Ta.

Strategy became a stream of infinite resources, that showered every cell in my being and thrust me to my feet— to rush into the moment when their group paused collectively.

I willed Khat to latch and pull up two corpses and secure them to the front and back of my body. When the last of the flesh of the corpse in front me was sealed to Khat, I had already dug my foot deep into the earth and sprung forward.

The sounds of clicking weaponry became dull and drawn-out in the distance. They would not catch me, I moved quicker than their insides could fire their movement.

Not even the added weight strapped against my body that drove my feet deeper into the earth and stressed the muscles in my legs could hinder my drive.

I joyfully welcomed the first volley of beams that pounded into their fallen comrades, forced me back in my steps and narrowly missed my flesh.

Their leader was mine.

An instinctive strike from their mistress swept past my head when I arrived in arm's length of her. While I rode it in on the inside of her arm, I spearhanded towards her throat. As I expected, she lowered her head and sought to run a fang into my fingers.

The heat of her breath and drool missed my hand when I yanked her loose hanging hair. When she panicked and reached upward to free herself, I shoved my hand into her chest and ripped out the heart, wrenching it from vessel and chord.

Our eyes met briefly before her head slumped on the shoulder of her comrade.

"Game over," I softly whispered into her ear and pushed her body away.

She hit the ground devoid of life. Would I meet the same fate as her? Falling to the foot of my enemy? Without fully knowing the reason why, I kneeled next to her while her people howled and called out scorns all around me.

I placed my hand over her eyes and closed them. A dense beam pounded hard into the corpse to my front and shook my hand away from her face.

I was out in the open.

One of the beams tore past my cheek and singed my skin––their aim improved over the last barrage of blasts. A bit of blood dripped from my cheek and into an open wound of the body sealed in the front of me. What started out as minor twitching, grew to it struggling against my body.

In one swift move, it swung its neck and snapped it around so it could face me. Fangs gnashed at me drawing dangerously close. After my instruction, Khat propelled it off me, yet it clawed desperately at me while it hurtled away from me.

Wasting no time, Khat rid me of the other although it seemed to not to present any danger. I charged forward barely escaping the beams that filled the air. Managing to time the trigger pulls and the heads of their shots left me with only a few burn marks around my body.

The first of their group I reached jerked back in surprise and fumbled about with the trigger of her blaster. Finally in frustration she turned her weapon around swung at me with the butt end.

Avoiding the last desperate blow with ease was one thing, being unable to pierce her chest with my counterstrike was another matter. Unlike the others who were unclothed and exposed, this frail and less athletic one was clad in some type of metallic suit that withstood my blow.

Seeing that I caused no harm she regained her wits and

jammed the weapon in my ribs. "Any last words before this blast has you? Your neck loo—"

Her words were too many and mouth wide enough to snatch out her jaw from her head.

Even though most of her face hung from lack of support and what was left of it bled profusely, she managed the strength to squeeze the trigger. The weapon fired at point blank range and Khat took most of the impact as well as siphoned off the tremendous heat.

Regardless of this, the suit remained intact. I dropped as if I was struck to the side by a hammer.

*I am spent and wanted nothing more than to rest and be done with this!*

A blast blazed passed my wounded side— instantly chased by another. I shifted away from them and was greeted by the agonizing sensation of cracked ribs scraped against my insides.

Bile shot in my throat while I collapsed to the ground, frantically pulling from sekhem in the recesses of my cells. Only to be met by Khat and my fertilized egg in my womb seeking nourishment in the same manner.

Through our rapport I came to realize that Khat could no longer draw upon vitality from the air unless it made my cells toxic with Esfet.

## N

*Let them have whatever they need...I will make due. I must… the Alde are close.*

Ignoring the potentially spirit crippling approach of their remaining numbers, I dragged my aching body along the ground towards the gun clutched in the still twitching hand. My limbs struggled to fight off the need to rest while my mind fought the irritation of that need.

When I forcefully pried the gun away, deathly coughs left her sloped hanging lips before she left her shell. As I wrapped the gun tight in my grasp and placed it underneath me, a soldier approached my side and kicked my leg.

I lay motionless, ignoring the secreted acid from the handle of the gun, experiencing neither anxiety nor silent rage, just patiently awaiting opportunity.

Her mistake was when she turned me over and revealed the barrel aimed at her chest. Despite the increasingly blistered flesh in my palm, three well place shots cracked through her sternum and left my trigger finger drained.

The others came rushing in as I clutched my chest from sharp pain brought on by Khat and my womb's pulling.

Undaunted by the thinning string that kept me attached to this world, wherever I heard and felt the break of air pressure I pointed the barrel and squeezed.

Bodies collapsed in all directions followed by others scattering about in the shadows, both sung out echoes in the chamber. Lack of strength was rapidly becoming a major issue as I watched it internally pulled away from me.

I pitifully tossed the gun only a few inches—thinking it traveled much further. Suddenly, my head rung with the blood curdling cries of Alde pleading for their lives, then moments later choking on it.

My senses spontaneously became sharper than usual and reverberated the grind and tear of flesh throughout my skull. It became all too painful to bare!

The will to fight stayed with me nevertheless the familiar scent of Jnfr that whirled about in the air was a comfort.

"Nth! *Nth!*" she called out to me.

My head weighed too heavy to look up right away, still I raised it and tilted it in her direction. It took a while for the blurriness to taper off before I could make out her form and another plowing into the Alde...

Towering bodies showing no mercy to the few that remained— the larger male with her, tore into them with a passionate fury.

All was over.

Esfet withdrew from here and the rays of the sun finally

peered through Apep's hole chasing away the agents of despair.

"Get her up and to the surface, *now!*" The urgency in Jnfr's voice partially shook her companion out of his frenzy.

He took me in his enormous arms and leapt out of the chamber in one bound.

*Never has the heat of a sun brought me so much elation, so much love!*

And the twin suns of their planet communicated that much more to my battle scarred body.

"Lay her in the clearing, for the eyes of Tn and R to see!" Jnfr spoke to the other.

He gently laid me down directly under the rays of their suns while I intuitively reached into Jnfr's mind. All was becoming clear about my reason for being on this world. *Those crafty Khenmenu Nebu...* "Since I have been on your world, I have not had a decent rest."

"Let me close my eyes for awhile. Then we will start." *Rest first. Then we wage our war.*

I closed my eyes and drifted soon after.

Listening to my child develop its heart...

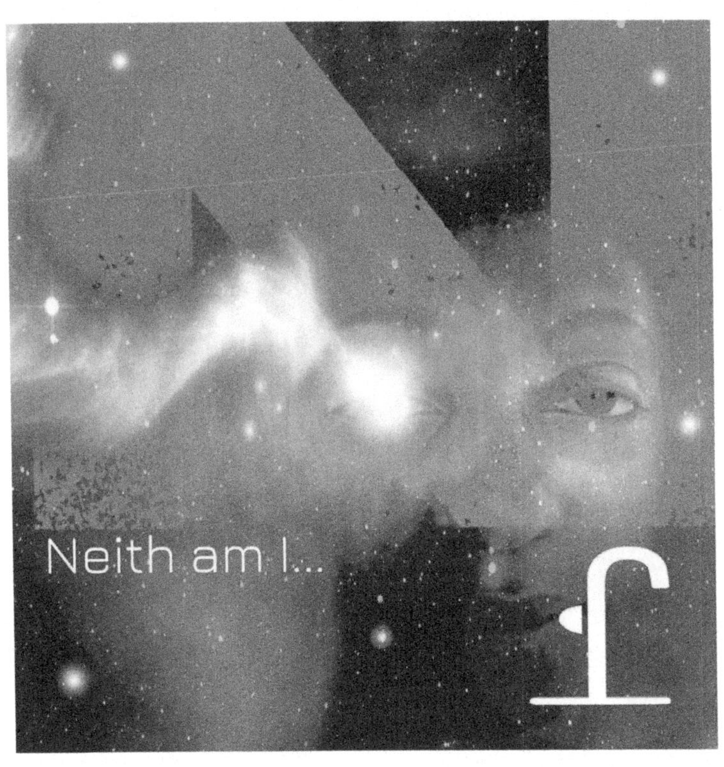
Neith am I...

N

# N

N

Made in the USA
Middletown, DE
07 January 2024

47197515R00179